Buffy rummaged  said, "A-ha!" She a squirt b

Giles blinked several times. "You intend to poison them with glass cleaner?"

"Hardly," Buffy said. She unscrewed the spray top of the bottle and dumped the blue liquid into a plastic bowl on the counter. "Dawn, I need you to find the butterfly net Dad got you when you were ten. Then bring all the holy water you can find in my room." Dawn ran for the stairs.

"I understand." Anya gave a nod of recognition. "You're making insecticide—or fairicide, in this case, I guess. I approve."

Spike turned from where he was looking through an upper cupboard. "Twisted. I like the way you think."

"Less talk," Buffy said, "more weapons."

Buffy the Vampire Slayer™

Available from SIMON PULSE

Little Things

Rebecca Moesta

**An original novel based on the hit television series
by Joss Whedon**

SIMON PULSE
NEW YORK LONDON TORONTO SYDNEY SINGAPORE

First Simon Pulse edition August 2002

TM and © 2002 Twentieth Century Fox Film Corporation.
All rights reserved.

SIMON PULSE
An imprint of Simon & Schuster
Children's Publishing Division
1230 Avenue of the Americas
New York, NY 10020

The text of this book was set in Times.
Printed in the United States of America.
2 4 6 8 10 9 7 5 3 1
The Library of Congress Control Number 2002105469
ISBN 0-7434-2736-X

This book is for two of my oldest (though by no means old) friends:

Lisa Jan Parker Chrisman,
who taught me to love fairies, even when they're a bit naughty
and
Ann Cathleen Hanna Neumann,
who knew long before I did what we wanted to be when we grew up

Thanks to both of you
for introducing me to some of the most magical books I've ever read

Acknowledgments

I'd like to express my special appreciation to:

Micol Ostow and Lisa Clancy, for giving me the opportunity, resources, and guidance to write this book.

Matt Bialer of the Trident Media Group, for taking care of the business end.

Diane E. Jones and Catherine Sidor of WordFire Inc., for their long hours and invaluable comments; Jonathan Cowan and Sarah L. Jones of WordFire Inc., for keeping things running smoothly in the office; and all of them for throwing themselves with such enthusiasm into absorbing Buffyology.

Maryelizabeth Hart, for suggesting that I dip my toe into the Buffy universe and Jeff Mariotte, for pretty much throwing me into the pool, when they found out I was a fan of the show. Thanks, guys.

My entire family, for checking up on me regularly to be sure I hadn't "fallen off" the writing wagon.

Joss Whedon and the cast and crew of *Buffy the Vampire Slayer,* for bringing to life such a terrific show.

Josh Ryan Evans, for standing in line to get my autograph all those years ago, even as his own career was finally taking off.

Dean and Gerda Koontz, for close to a decade of good business advice.

Deb Ray, for her years of encouragement, both close up and long-distance. You're never far from my heart.

Cherie Buchheim, the Research Goddess I most admire.

Shannon and Linda Lifchez, for their indomitable cheerfulness and uncanny ability to make me feel special. (Yes, you too, James.)

Noël and Summer Chrisman, and Anyssa and Ambria Neumann for offering living proof that the potential and promise of the next generation is everything your mothers and I hoped it would be.

Sarah and Dan Hoyt, and Becky and Alan Lickiss for local cheerleading.

Leslie Lauderdale, for urging me to "go slay another chapter."

Denise Jacobs, for understanding, as only a working mother can, when I needed a little time alone.

Joe Cooper and Chris Willis, for their research on the Cottingley fairies.

Brian Herbert and Gregory Benford, for presenting Kevin with enough testosterone challenges to keep him happily writing for years. (You're maniacs, the lot of you.)

Doug Beason, for making sure I didn't forget that a writer writes.

And last, but never least, Kevin J. Anderson, for all the love, encouragement, and support a wife and fellow writer could ever hope for.

Prologue

The warm Santa Ana winds blew through Southern California for three days, carrying with them a roiling cloud of dirt, leaves, twigs, and fast-food wrappers. In Sunnydale the invisible destructive currents tore limbs from trees, sent garbage cans rolling through the streets, scattering their contents all the way, rattled windows, banged screen doors, and upended patio tables. Toward the end of the third day, the windstorm died down, leaving the skies a sunny blue scoured clean of all haze.

But the wind left something behind. . . .

Cherie Beeheim waited alone in Weatherly Park beneath an old oak tree in the gathering dusk. Tonight was going to be magical, and she let herself enjoy the anticipation. At the sound of crunching footsteps she whirled to look behind her, but nobody was there. She saw a flicker of movement from the corner of her eye and turned toward it. Again nothing.

"Boo!"

Cherie shrieked and turned back to find that Josh had managed to sneak around the far side of the tree to surprise her. She guessed he must have come straight from the Kent Prep School basketball practice, because his hair was damp and he carried a small Hilfiger gym duffel. Her heart raced at the sight of Joshua Norton Clarke III, a handsome prep-school senior and her date for the night. Dressed in wallet-draining designer casuals, he was tall and muscular with clear blue eyes and sandy hair. Definite hunkage material, if ever there was. He flashed her that confident I-had-two-years-of-braces smile, a smile so perfect it could jitter the stomach of any high-school girl, including Cherie. Including his preppy girlfriend, Cara Crandall. Cherie smothered a flash of irritation at the thought of her rival. Spoiled rich girl.

Magical, Cherie reminded herself. *Tonight is going to be just perfect.* After all, hadn't she changed out of her St. Michael's school uniform and worn her hottest dress? Low-cut and sleeveless, all drapey and flowy in ruby silk, the mini was guaranteed to make any red-blooded guy forget that other girls even existed on the planet. And the last thing Cherie wanted Josh to do right now was think about other girls.

"Happy to see me?" Josh asked.

She tossed her long dark hair and fluttered her eyelashes at him. "I'll have to think of a way to punish you for scaring me like that," she teased.

He gave her his patented smile again. "I think I can make it up to you. Come on." He grabbed her hand. "Let's walk."

Cherie let herself be led away from the oak tree, away from the pathways, deeper into the park. A few stray gusts of wind swirled the leaves around their feet as they left streetlights behind and pushed into the deepening shadows. They passed gnarled old trees that cast ghoulish silhouettes against the clear evening sky. Something glimmered briefly at the edge of her vision. She ignored it. Josh was all that mattered right now.

Cherie's pulse raced—not with fear, but with the excitement of The Forbidden. Her father thought she was still studying at the library. But after only an hour of homework Cherie had changed clothes, put on her makeup, and hurried from the library to Weatherly Park. Now here she was, walking across the grass after dark—she, who had never dared to leave the paved paths before—with a boy who was, strictly speaking, not her boyfriend . . . yet.

When Joshua stopped abruptly between a pair of dense bushes and began to kiss her, Cherie did not pretend to object. This was the magic moment she had been hoping for. Confident that they were completely alone and there was no chance someone would come upon them by accident, the two kissed. Time lost all meaning for them as they wrapped their arms around each other, pressing as close as two human beings could while still fully clothed. By the time they pulled apart panting for breath, a large, nearly full moon was peeking at them through the screening branches. A full moon might have been slightly *more* perfect of course, but Cherie wasn't about to complain.

She gave a sigh of pleasure. "Very romantic."

Apparently taking this as a personal compliment, Josh said, "Wait. It gets better." He picked up the small gym duffel he had brought with him and rummaged around in it for a moment before producing a faded yellow beach towel, which he spread on the tiny patch of open ground at their feet. "If zee mademoiselle would seet, please?" he said in his best Pepe Le Pew French accent, pointing down toward the beach towel.

She sat, careful to show plenty of leg as she did so. Her legs were two of her best features. Something caught her eye. The barest hint of movement. She looked up to see a bush shaking where Josh had bumped it with his elbow. *Relax. Don't be so jumpy,* she told herself. *He'll think you're a total newbie at this date stuff.* Which, of course, was true. But he didn't need to know that.

After taking a few more things from the bag, Josh sat down beside her. "Eh, *voilà!*" he announced, grinning triumphantly. By the uncertain moonlight, she could see that he held a screw-top bottle of red wine and two small drinking glasses. Kids' glasses, to be more exact—of the kind that usually come filled with grape jelly.

Wine. There it was again: The Forbidden. At eighteen, Josh was closer to legal drinking age than Cherie, who had turned sixteen only two weeks ago. She knew her father wouldn't approve, but Cherie felt the most amazing warm tingle at the pit of her stomach, and she firmly squelched all thoughts of caution. Anyway, she hadn't gotten all glammed up for the evening just for nothing. Whatever happened, she knew that tonight would change her life forever.

He handed her a cup with a picture of Wilma Flintstone on it, and she held it out while he filled it to the brim with crimson wine. Watching him pour the second glass of wine, Cherie suddenly found herself nervous. The Wilma glass shook in her hand and she took a huge gulp, as much to keep it from overflowing as to cover her attack of nerves. Josh refilled her glass, took a drink from his Bam-Bam Rubble cup, then leaned forward and pressed his damp lips to hers.

Cherie's eyes had fallen half shut, so she barely saw it at the edge of her vision. "Oh!" She sat up straight and drew in a sharp breath.

"What? What is it?" Josh said.

"I . . . I thought I saw a firefly. I love fireflies. I see them every summer when I go out to spend Fourth of July in Wisconsin with my aunt, but—"

"But it's not summer, and we don't have fireflies in California," Josh finished for her.

"Right." She shrugged and took a few more sips of wine.

"Could be someone carrying one of those little pocket flashlights," Josh said, sounding irritated at the idea of an interruption. "I'd better go check and see if—"

"Wait. There it is again." Cherie pointed. "And another one." Just above the nearest bush a pair of tiny lights alternately glowed, grew brighter, winked out, and then flashed on again.

"What the . . . ," Josh said in a low voice. He put down his glass and got slowly to his feet. Another light winked on behind him, then one beside his shoulder.

"Listen," Cherie said. From somewhere nearby came a faint buzzing sound, almost like the ominous humming of a bee in flight, yet more musical somehow.

Then all of a sudden the little lights were all around them, glowing brightly, and Cherie could see what they were. She gasped. The half-empty cup of wine slipped from her fingers and splashed its blood-red contents onto the pale beach towel, but Cherie hardly noticed. A tiny, perfectly formed creature hovered in front of her face. The miniature woman was beautiful and looked absolutely human—except that she was no bigger than Cherie's index finger, and from her back sprouted two pair of delicate, gossamer ovals that fluttered as fast as a hummingbird's wings. The tiny thing wore a diaphanous dress of spring green that perfectly matched her eyes, and her flowing golden hair radiated light that cast a sort of spherical halo around her petite figure.

"A . . . a fairy?" Cherie whispered. "It *is* magical."

"Just like Tinkerbell," Josh said. "There must be twenty of them."

Slowly, ever so slowly, so as not to frighten them away, Cherie raised a hand, palm down, until it was between her face and the minute golden nymph. As if with utmost caution, the glowing creature drifted forward, touched down lightly on the hand for just a second, and flitted away again. Then Cherie heard a new sound, like sprinkles of microscopic laughter.

Three of the fairies, glowing gold, silver, and apricot, flew around Cherie's head, tugging lightly at her hair. They took turns lifting wisps of hair and playfully tossing them across her face. She giggled with delight. Then, to her amazement, they each grasped a few strands and wove back and forth around each other until the hair was plaited in a flawless slender braid.

Josh chuckled as well. "Hey, catch this. One of them landed on me."

Cherie got carefully to her feet and giggled softly when she saw the little raven-haired creature perched on his ear, shining like a tiny black light. Moments later, close to a dozen of the little fairies encircled her and put on a display of complex aerobatic maneuvers as they flew slowly around and around. Maybe the wine had begun to affect her, or maybe it was part of the magic of the evening, but Cherie realized she couldn't look away.

A second circle of winged sprites formed around Josh, and the two teens watched, mesmerized. Enchanted. The evening took on an otherworldly quality, and for a moment Cherie was tempted to think that she and Josh had fallen asleep on the beach towel and were simply dreaming. But she would never have dreamed something like this, would she?

"They're dancing for us," Josh whispered.

"It's beautiful," Cherie agreed. Even to her own ears, her voice sounded dreamy and distant. Strange, she hadn't noticed it till now, but gradually the dancing fairies had sped up and drawn their circles tighter, until they were nearly touching Cherie and Josh as they flew in fast circles at shoulder level. The dancing grew wilder, less organized, and Cherie found that she could barely track their movements. She stared straight ahead, completely captivated. They fluttered and dodged in and out of her view. Cherie began to feel dizzy. One of the fairies, a tiny man with cherry-red hair and a fawn-colored jerkin, came to rest on her shoulder. Charming, yet she felt a spider of apprehension crawl up her spine. Then . . .

"Ouch." She heard a slapping sound from Josh's direction. "Hey . . . I think one of them stung me—or *bit* me." Strangely, though, his voice was warm and languid. He didn't sound at all alarmed.

Cherie shook her head and tried to blink the haze from her eyes. With her vision clear, she could see that the beautiful little creatures looked different now. A spider web of dark veins crisscrossed their formerly translucent wings. The miniature faces no longer looked human. Their foreheads were ridged and lumpy, and their open mouths revealed long, needle-sharp fangs. A stinging at the base of her bare neck made Cherie shiver. She touched the spot.

Wet.

She looked at her fingers and saw with vague interest that there was blood on them. It didn't matter. The night was magical.

More stinging. Josh moaned but didn't cry out again. Cherie tried to move, then forgot why she had wanted to.

The swarm closed in around her.

Chapter One

The Magic Box was filled with most of the things that were comforting in Buffy's life: her sister, her Watcher, her best friends in the world (except for Xander, who was working late), warm light, old books, and all the magicky stuff that the shop sold. She had finished her training for the day and changed into street clothes. She should have felt perfectly comfortable, but some vague pain was irritating her, and she couldn't put her finger on it.

In general, pain was pretty much irrelevant to Slayers; fortunately they recovered quickly from most injuries they sustained during training or fighting. She gave a mental shrug. Whatever was wrong, it would probably heal itself quickly enough.

Buffy joined her friends at the table in the main room of the Magic Box. Giles, satisfied that he had discharged his watcherly duties for the day, was busy unpacking a shipment of artifacts and magical paraphernalia that had just arrived. Tara, Willow, and Dawn were already at the table, while Anya stood behind the sales counter, eagerly totaling the day's receipts for the shop. This was Anya's first real job since losing her thousand-year vengeance-demon gig, and Buffy was often surprised at the ex-demon, hundred-percent-human girl's passion and aptitude for business.

A fairly serious discussion was already under way when Buffy sat down. "Looks like frowny-face is in order," she observed. "What gives?"

Willow gave Dawn a gentle nudge. "Tell her."

Buffy snagged a carrot stick from a plastic sandwich bag at the center of the table and sat back. "Listening."

"I can't. Buffy'll be mad at me," Dawn whispered to Willow. She looked over at her sister. "Promise you won't be mad at me."

Buffy's stomach tightened. This wasn't a promising start. Since their mother's recent death, Buffy was still unsure of when to be sisterly or when to act motherly. She couldn't guarantee how she would respond. "Still listening," Buffy said. "Mind open."

Dawn fidgeted, then also grabbed a carrot stick from the sandwich bag and bit down on it. Not quite meeting Buffy's eyes, she said, "I'm not doing as well as I'd like to in history, and there's a big test coming up on Tuesday."

Anya put down the receipts she was adding, looked with helpful concern across the counter at

Buffy, and spoke in a low voice. "Dawn is getting a D-plus right now."

Considering this new information, Buffy bit down on her carrot stick and began to chew thoughtfully. A jolt of pain arced through her jaw and seemed to jump all the way to the top of her skull. She gasped and rocked back from the table, almost choking on a bit of carrot. Her tooth! That's what had been bothering her. It had been sensitive and irritated for a couple of days. Believing that it would soon heal on its own, Buffy had managed to ignore the discomfort, as she so often did, but now it was an all-out ache. What if a Slayer's powers of quick healing didn't apply to teeth? Buffy realized with a sinking feeling that she and Dawn had no dental insurance, and now that Buffy had dropped her college classes, she was no longer eligible to go to the college health center. She pressed her lips together. Too bad that being the Chosen One didn't come with a benefit plan. Buffy didn't want to worry Dawn. She would tough it out. The throbbing ache would go away. It had to.

"See? I *told* you she was going to be mad at me," Dawn said to Tara and Willow. "Why did you make me tell her?"

"Well, she's your sister. She . . . she needs to know these things," Willow pointed out. "Buffy, please don't be mad at her."

Buffy shook her head, trying to will away the pain. "No, not mad. Pretty unthrilled that I'm the last to know, of course. Mostly, I'm disappointed." She chose her next words more carefully. "School is . . . is . . . important. At mid-semester a D-plus isn't an emergency, it's just a . . . an indicator, a red flag, right? No big. But we've got to deal. I mean, it's only a little pothole at the moment, but it could become a great big sinkhole—in which you would, uh . . . sink. So we just need to do something before it gets worse. Okay?"

Dawn nodded. "Monday's a teacher workday, so I've got a three-day weekend to study."

"Good," Buffy said. "We can't let a little problem become a big problem. After all, this is Problem Solver Central, right?"

"Sure," Willow said. "And Tara and I, we can help her study."

Tara smiled. "That sounds fun. We were going to hang out at the Bronze tonight, but we can do that anytime. Dawn is much more important. We could start right away." A sense of relief rose in Buffy.

"Ah. Sounds like the perfect solution, Buffy," Giles said, unwrapping an envelope of seeds that had come in today's shipment of specialty items. According to the packing slip, the seeds came from a peculiar plant that has belonged to an infamous Danish vampire. "And if Tara and Willow need a break, I could always lend a hand. Unless of course, it's an obscure bit of American history . . . ?"

Dawn shook her head. "The Colonial Period."

Giles's eyebrows went up. "Oh? Excellent. It's all settled, then. Problem solved." He laid out neat rows of each kind of incense he was taking out of the box.

"Well, it's a start anyway." Buffy had been a bit

shaky herself on the whole history thing during high school and wasn't sure she would be a big help to Dawn. But Willow and Tara loved history. And Giles— well, Giles practically lived with his nose in a history book. Still, Buffy was Dawn's sister and felt like she ought to lend some kind of support.

A bell jingled as the shop door opened, and Xander walked in and scuffed down the three steps into the main retail room. Anya came out from behind the counter and greeted him with an enthusiastic kiss. "Giles and I made $736.22 today."

Xander flashed a grin at his friends, then looked into Anya's eyes with a mock serious expression. "Now, Ahn, we talked about this, didn't we?"

Anya thought, brightened, then said as if reciting, "I had an extremely successful day at work, financially speaking. How was your day, Xander?"

Xander smiled graciously. "Stunk. Spent ten and a half hours fixing flashing and replacing roof tiles that were damaged by the windstorm. Our construction schedule's shot. I'm redoing work that I already did last week. And yet, no one to blame. You can't fight the wind."

Willow pressed her lips together in a sympathetic expression. "Frustrating."

"Big time," Xander agreed. "So I'm thinking to myself, what's the best way to get rid of a little pent up aggression?"

Anya blinked. "I understand. Although I still have some work to do, I suppose I could take a break and—"

"Whoa—who's for patrolling?" Xander cut in.

Buffy hesitated. "We were kind of working out a solution to a little problem."

"Which, actually, we pretty much did," Willow pointed out. "Don't worry, Buffy. Dawn's in good hands."

"I know." Buffy gave her friend a wry smile. "Didn't you get me through high school?"

"I'll order a pizza," Tara said. "We can eat while we study, and then we'll walk Dawn home."

"Thanks. You guys are the best," Buffy said, then looked at Xander. "Okay, I'm in."

"Yeah, I kind of figured," Xander said. "Anyone else? Ahn, want to come with?" Xander asked. "A little bit of healthy slayage to top off the day?"

"I still have work to finish. I need to calculate sales tax totals for our quarterly report. Then I have to update our Web site to add the new inventory. You two go ahead and enjoy yourselves. I'll meet you at home in a couple of hours. After all, you left so early this morning, we didn't really have a chance for—"

"—for dessert," Xander cut in quickly. "After breakfast. I had to get to work early today to fix that roof that was damaged by the wind."

"Dessert?" Dawn seemed intrigued by the concept. "*I* don't get dessert after breakfast."

"Well, what about pancakes?" Buffy said. "That's like dessert."

"Ooh, or waffles," Willow added.

"And I suppose scones with clotted cream might be considered a sort of dessert," Giles offered. A glint of amusement showed in his hazel eyes. He carefully set aside a matched trio of focusing crystals he had unpacked. "Although, I must say I rather prefer them at tea time instead."

"There's donuts. Or toaster pastries," Tara said.

"See?" Buffy smiled at her sister. "Throw in some sweetened cereal and a few cheese Danish and you pretty much have a whole dessert fest in the morning."

Anya gave them all a how-dense-can-you-be look. "Xander wasn't talking about food," she said helpfully. "He meant the sex."

Xander sighed, lowered his head, and pinched the bridge of his nose as if suddenly overcome by a tension headache. "Subtlety, thy name is *anything* but Anya."

Buffy pulled on a cropped leather jacket. The early spring evening wasn't cold, but she often wore leather to keep from getting quite as scraped up when, in the course of normal business, demons and vamps decided to throw her against walls or stomp her into the dirt. Trying to ignore her still-aching tooth, she picked up a couple of stakes and stuffed them into her pockets. "Okay, time to get back to your history," she told Dawn in a firm voice.

While Xander collected a stake and a crossbow, Buffy turned to Anya. "I'll have junk-food boy home in plenty of time for dessert." Then to Xander, "Let's rock."

Chapter Two

After leaving the Magic Box, Buffy and Xander grabbed a couple of burgers and headed out on patrol. Although Buffy ate quickly and chewed only on the side that didn't hurt, by the time she finished, her tooth was throbbing worse than ever, and she shared Xander's need to take out a little bit of aggression on something. They had walked less than a mile before trouble found them.

A pair of Tyrloch demons emerged from the shadows in the cemetery and confronted them. The demons had mottled, greenish-blue skin, bulging muscles, and a row of straight, sharp horns sprouting from their foreheads.

Xander assessed them with interest. "So . . . now we know what it would look like if the Incredible Hulk and the Statue of Liberty ever had kids."

One of the Tyrlochs growled and raised his six-fingered hands in a threatening gesture. A four-inch talon sprang from the end of each digit.

"Just so we're perfectly clear," Buffy said, holding up a cautioning finger, "are you evil, or is this just some sort of tragic failure to communicate?"

There was the barest hint of insincerity in Xander's voice as he said, "'Cause we'd really *hate* to kill you over a misunderstanding." He held his crossbow at the ready and flexed his free hand.

The taller of the two demons lunged, claws outstretched. Xander shot an arrow that went wild as the Tyrloch bore him to the ground. Xander smashed at the demon's hands with the crossbow, shattering several talons.

"You should try the acrylics," Buffy said conversationally. "They're really quite reasonable—not to mention a stand-out fashion statement." She was ready for the second demon. When it sprang at her, she threw herself to one side and mule kicked it as it tumbled past. She turned before it could regain its feet and went on the offensive with a kick to its chin. The Tyrloch used the momentum to tuck into a backward somersault and pop up in a defensive crouch. Buffy could hear Xander and the first demon tussling, but the sounds seemed far away. When she spared a glance in her friend's direction, she saw that Xander was nearly a block away.

Buffy's opponent chose that unguarded second to bound forward and catch her with an open-handed wallop to the side of her face. Agony exploded from her tooth and she spun and reeled, temporarily blinded by the pain. She tried to strike back with a right cross and missed.

Apparently as surprised as she was, the demon took advantage of her disorientation. It grabbed her and tossed her in reverse down the sidewalk. She skidded ten feet along the concrete on her back in her leather jacket. Trying to gather her wits, she pushed up to a kneeling position and grumbled, "Being a slayer sure is tough on the wardrobe."

The Tyrloch made a flying leap for her, taloned hands spread, dagger-toothed mouth open wide. Buffy reacted on sheer instinct. She pulled a stake from her pocket with one hand and fell backward, supporting herself with the other. When the jaws were less than a foot from her face, Buffy plunged her stake through the creature's open mouth and deep into its throat. The demon exploded into several gallons of smelly blue-green goo. Panting, Buffy got to her feet and wiped globs of Tyrloch slime from her clothes.

A voice just behind her left ear said, "Out of baddies so soon? Pity."

Spike.

Buffy whirled, trying not to show her annoyance at how thoroughly he had surprised her. The sardonic blond vampire should not have been able to sneak up on her so easily. "What are you doing here?" she demanded, and clamped her teeth in anger—an action she instantly regretted, as another lightning bolt of pain struck her tooth.

Spike gave her a knowing smirk. "Tooth hurts,

does it, love? Are you simply being macho, or do you find that the pain helps you fight?"

"Neither," Buffy snapped, irritated that he had already noticed the chink in her armor when none of her other friends had. "It's nothing I can't handle. Anyway, even if I wanted to I couldn't go to a dentist. Mom didn't have dental insurance, and I'm not a student anymore." Then, as if realizing she'd just told him more than she'd told anyone else, she added for good measure, "Not that it's any of your business." To her chagrin, she saw a softening look on the vampire's face.

"Insurance or not, you need to get that fixed, love." Spike flashed her a rueful smile. "We all need our teeth, don't we? And it could get much worse. Got to take care of yourself if you're going to save the world."

"Save the . . . Oh!" Buffy looked around in alarm. "Xander?"

Spike shook his head. "Wouldn't worry about that one. Been watching you both, but neither of you seemed to need any help. Actually seemed to be enjoying himself, Xander did."

"You've been *spying* on us? Of all the weasely, fang-faced, parasitic—"

"I've got something to show you," Spike said in a quiet voice.

"Like what? Your etchings?" Buffy scoffed. "Or maybe you brought in some new bones to redecorate your crypt. No, thanks."

Spike didn't rise to the bait. "No, it's in Weatherly Park. Something *you* need to see. As the Slayer. Bit more interesting than this lot."

A hoot of triumph echoed through the night, and Xander came bounding up to Buffy, a gleeful grin on his face. "Demons, take a number. The Xan Man is on a roll." Then, spotting Spike, he said, "And the line forms here."

Buffy sighed and shook her head. "Maybe later, Xander. Right now he's here on business." She shot Spike a dangerous look. "And this better be good."

Spike gave her an ambiguous half-smile. "Thought you should see it before the cops carted the bodies off."

Chapter Three

It was a short, brisk walk to Weatherly Park with Buffy setting the pace. She was determined to find out what Spike had gotten his fangs in a twist about. In all likelihood, he wouldn't leave her alone until then. She found the very thought of working with him distasteful, especially since Spike had decided he had the warm fuzzies for her. But she had to admit that he had been helpful more times than she could count now, and she couldn't afford to ignore him completely. Learning to deal with people, especially dead people, was just one of the challenges she had accepted as part of her slayer duties.

Even though she liked to stay ahead of Spike both mentally and physically, she had no idea what he had brought her here to see, so she stopped at the edge of the park and gestured for him to lead. "Your party."

Here and there streetlamps melted the night, leaving warm yellow puddles of light around the park. Spike's black leather trench coat fluttered like a dark moth as he led them away from the path.

When they got to a cluster of bushes in a quiet section of the park, Spike ducked between two of the bushes, and Buffy and Xander squeezed through after him. Xander's reaction to what he saw was instant. "Whoa! Are they—"

"Dead, yeah. I checked," Spike said.

Buffy stared down at the ground, trying to understand what she was seeing. By the light of the almost full moon, she could tell that a couple was lying on a pale piece of cloth on the dark ground. Tiny dark spots marred the skin at their throats, wrists, and temples, and at the girl's knees and ankles on her bare legs. "Do you have a light?" Buffy asked of no one in particular, kneeling down to get a better look. She heard a snicking sound and a cigarette lighter appeared in the air about a foot above the male victim's face. Buffy shot Spike a withering look. "That's *it?*"

"Photon man to the rescue," Xander said, producing a flashlight. "Be prepared. I learned that in the Boy Scouts in the oh-so-brief time they allowed me to be a member."

Spike took out a cigarette, lit it, and put the lighter back in his pocket. Xander turned the flashlight on and held the beam so that it illuminated both bodies.

The girl was pretty in a dark and exotic sort of way, as if she might have played Mata Hari in an old film. The boy was tall and high-school-jock handsome, though not remarkable in any other way.

Buffy slowly shook her head. Every time she thought she had seen everything and couldn't be surprised anymore, she discovered she was wrong. The small spots and smears she had seen on the bodies turned out to be tiny wounds and dribbles of blood. But it didn't look like there was enough blood loss to kill them. Buffy touched the girl's neck, feeling for a pulse. There was none, but the body was still warm. An hour earlier and she might have been able to save her, but Buffy had been oblivious to whatever had caused this. Had she let a little thing like a toothache interfere with her slayer radar? Impossible. At least she hoped so. She turned her frustration on Spike.

"Okay, so you brought me here to show me what, that some sort of murderous pest is on the loose now? As if Sunnydale doesn't have enough trouble with vampires, demons, and the occasional werewolf, now we have giant mosquitoes? Did you ever consider that this might not be a job for the Slayer? Maybe we just need an exterminator."

"Hold on, Pet. Don't stake the messenger." Spike held up his hands in a defensive gesture. "Whole situation's wonky, and you know it."

He was right. Still, Buffy was not ready to give him the satisfaction of admitting it yet. This wasn't about Spike, though. It was about death, about protecting the innocent. She let her slayer instincts kick in. "Do we know who they are?"

"Not by name," Xander answered, "but the girl looks familiar. I think Willow knows her."

Spike blew out a puff of smoke from his cigarette. "We could check for IDs."

"You haven't even looked yet?" Buffy asked, incredulous.

Spike shrugged. "Didn't want you accusing me of trying to steal from the dead."

"Did you see what happened?" Buffy said.

Spike shook his head. "Found them like that 'bout half an hour ago."

Buffy leaned closer to get a better look at the wounds, dozens of paired, pin-prick fine holes. "I think we can rule out drugs," she observed wryly. "And if these were poisonous insect stings, there should be swelling."

"Right," Spike agreed. "And that wouldn't explain the loss of blood."

Buffy touched one of the puncture wounds. "It doesn't look like they've lost much, a few drops here and there."

"What about this?" Xander said, pointing to a dark patch on the towel that the couple lay on.

"Naw, burgundy," Spike said with a derisive snort. "Bottled circa . . . last month, I'd say."

Xander picked up the Wilma Flintstone cup and sniffed it. "Say what you will, but I've got to admire the man's taste in stemware—though I'm actually more of a Betty Rubble man, myself. What's this?" He bent over a small duffel, looked through it, and held up a handful of condoms. "And I'd always heard these went better with a cheap white zinfandel."

Buffy sighed. "Candy is dandy . . ."

"Well, whoever this guy was, he wasn't poor," Xander observed.

"Oh, how do you figure?" Although Xander and the blond-haired vampire were usually at odds with each other, Spike sounded intrigued in spite of himself.

Xander considered. "Well, there's the shoes for starters—not to mention the rest of his clothes. Let's see. Cross-trainers: a hundred and forty dollars. Designer jeans: a hundred and sixty. Warm-up vest: ninety. T-shirt: sixty-five. . . . Beating heart? Priceless."

"So?" Spike said. "They're dead *and* rich."

"Not the girl," Xander corrected. "Dress is designer knock-off, strictly off-the-rack, eighty bucks max."

"And you know this . . . how?" Buffy said, looking up at him with a strange expression.

"How long did I date Cordelia Chase?"

"Point taken."

Xander picked up a postage-stamp-sized purse from beside the girl. "Not much here. Just a house key, brand new driver's license, two dollars, a quarter, and some lip gloss. Cherie Beeheim, just turned sixteen. Definitely not from the same side of the financial tracks as Prince Jock."

Spike crouched down by the boy's body for a moment, retrieved something from a pocket, looked at it briefly, then slapped it down in front of Buffy. "Joshua Norton Clarke III," he said. He glanced at Xander with reluctant approval. "Looks like Sidekick Boy got it right."

Because she knew Spike was watching, Buffy looked through the wallet. "School ID says he's a senior at Kent Prep." Everything else seemed to be there, too: money, a credit card, driver's license, and a school photo of a blond-haired girl that was dated only a few days earlier and signed, *All my love, Cara.* She handed it to Xander. "Take a look."

He gave a low whistle. "So, Josh's night out without the girlfriend, huh?"

"Hoping for an evening of secret smoochies—and then some," Buffy confirmed.

Xander made a sound of disgust. "That explains a lot. Cheap son-of-a b—"

"But that doesn't explain how they died," Buffy said.

"Doesn't have to be anything supernatural," Xander said. "Could just be the work of an incompetent acupuncturist."

Buffy looked at the unnaturally pale faces of the dead couple—who weren't really a couple—then glanced at Spike. "Are you sure they've lost that much blood?"

Spike put a hand on the dead girl's ankle. "She's down a liter, maybe more." He nodded toward the boy. "Same for Don Juan junior, I'd guess."

Buffy shook her head. "Vampires I understand, but not this."

"So you think this could be the work of a jealous girlfriend?" Xander asked.

"Sure," Spike said sarcastically. "Maybe if she's a phlebotomist and withdrew their blood into a hundred syringes. No, wait—she would have had to chloroform them first."

"I don't hear you making any suggestions, Bleach Brain," Xander said. "If you think this is supernatural, how 'bout this? Maybe it was the work of a rogue stapler. Or maybe these kids fell victim to a band of roving hamster-sized demon worshippers who needed a ritual sacrifice."

Buffy blew out a frustrated breath and stood up. She looked straight at Spike. She didn't want to give him the idea that she was grateful to him or in any way indebted. He reminded her of a cat bringing its master a dead bird. And Buffy didn't need any more dead birds than she already had. "Okay, I'll ask Giles what he makes of all this. But don't hold your breath. Yes, two people died here tonight in a mysterious and . . . and icky way. But I'm not sure this is slayer territory."

"But the missing blood—"

"I *said* I'll ask Giles. Xander and I have a patrol to finish."

Spike stuffed his hands into his pockets. "Suit yourself then."

Buffy squeezed back between the bushes. "Come on, Xander. Let's go."

As she walked away, a vague uneasy feeling built within her. Xander, who knew her too well, said, "Spidey senses tingling?"

Buffy grimaced, then nodded. "Yeah, we'd better take a look around the park."

Xander grinned. "I've got your back."

Chapter Four

Willow Rosenberg was in her element. If ever an activity had been designed with her in mind, it was gathering and sharing knowledge. The past two hours had seemed to whiz by in a blur of pizza and early colonial history.

Dawn sighed, picked up the pizza box, and took it to the trash. "In a weird way, that was actually interesting."

Willow beamed. "Giles and Tara and I do make an impressive tutorial tag team, if I do say so myself."

"And what about me?" Anya said from behind the counter where she was affixing a stamp to a large squarish envelope. "I participated as well."

"Of course," Willow said, trying to hide her smile as she remembered Anya's contributions. "I especially liked the part where you explained what really happened to the lost Roanoke Colony. Kinda puts things in a whole new perspective."

"Indeed," Giles agreed, turning out the lights in the back room. "Who knew that vengeance demons got about quite that much?"

Dawn returned to the table and started putting her schoolbooks into her backpack. "You were all great," she said. "Really."

Tara helped Dawn put on her backpack. "We could talk some more while Willow and I walk you home," she offered.

"Sounds good," Dawn said. Willow opened the shop door, jingling the bell.

"Good night," Giles said.

"I trust you had an adequate educational experience," Anya said, and Dawn, Tara, and Willow trooped out into the night.

Before either of the wiccans could bring up a subject, Dawn said, "So what was school like for you guys? I mean, were you always like the perfect students?"

"Oh no, of course not. Not perfect," Willow said. "I mean there was that time I got a C on my trig exam. Of course, I'd had the flu for a week, and there was this ucky sinus thing, but—oh, not helping, huh?"

Tara self-consciously tucked her hair back behind her ear. "I was a good student," she admitted, "but my family was a mess and I didn't have very many friends. I mostly kept to myself. I wasn't very happy." Willow gave her a comforting hug, and Tara added, "But that was before I came here. I'm happy now."

Dawn groaned. "So I have to wait until college before life gets any easier?"

At the end of the block they turned the corner and headed into a residential district. Willow sighed. "When I was your age I was like this total geek. There wasn't that much to my life other than schoolwork. And Xander was my friend, but I wasn't exactly a member of the popular crowd, if you know what I mean. So that's not so perfect. It wasn't until my sophomore year when Buffy transferred to Sunnydale High that I sort of found my niche and learned to enjoy it. I decided that keeping the world safe from evily stuff was way more important than being popular. Plus, I had Buffy and Xander and Giles, and sometimes even Cordelia and Angel. . . ."

"School is important," Tara said quietly, "but friends are even more important. They can get you through anything."

"Right," Willow said. "And everybody messes up now and then. But a real friend won't just let you, you know, go down the drain."

"Which is why you're helping me with history," Dawn said.

"Right. Because we're your friends," Willow said.

"Smart friends," Dawn said. "Plus, I like that you're all cool and magickal and stuff."

They walked along in companionable silence for a few minutes, past lampposts, cozy homes, palm trees, and picket fences, until Dawn suddenly stopped in her tracks, staring with her mouth partly open. Willow and Tara stopped too.

"Did you see it?" Dawn whispered.

Willow looked in the direction the younger girl was staring. A glow appeared in midair above a rose bush near the darkened two-story house they were passing. The light disappeared, then reappeared closer to them, bobbing gently like a leaf floating on the surface of a rippling pond.

"Is that a—" Tara began.

"A fairy," Dawn said.

"Ookay, now I've officially seen everything."

The hovering light stopped right in front of them, then flitted back and forth before the three girls as if it was just as curious about them as they were about it. Dawn held her index finger parallel to the ground and moved it slowly toward the fairy, as if she were trying to coax a bird. An apricot glow surrounded the creature in its sheer teal dress.

"It's a girl, just like Tinkerbell," Willow said. The beautiful creature darted out of reach.

"Shhh," Dawn said. "Don't scare it."

The fairy flew in agitated circles over their heads for a few seconds, then gradually made a slow spiral toward Dawn's finger. The younger girl's eyes reflected the glow of the fairy light with a look of absolute amazement.

"I can't believe it," Willow said. "Usually when something new and, you know, mythological, comes to Sunnydale, it's something really uch, like a demon or a ghost even. It's nice to know that there's something beautiful in the world, like fairies."

Just then, the fairy reached Dawn's finger, but it did not perch on it as they had all expected. Instead, it bit down hard. The transformation had been so quick that none of them had had the chance to react. "Ouch," Dawn said, shaking the fairy away as if it were a bee that had just stung her. The fairy flitted up and out of sight. "It went all fang-facey."

"Are you all right?" Tara asked, pulling a tissue from her pocket and wrapping it around Dawn's finger.

"Figures," Willow said. "We couldn't just get some normal fairies in Sunnydale?"

Dawn unwrapped the tissue and peered down at her finger. "Doesn't look too bad."

"Uh-oh. Incoming," Willow said, pointing to a spot just above the wooden gate that led to the backyard of the house. Several of the fairies were working together to grasp and lift a small wriggling bundle of curly black fur.

"But what is it?" Tara asked. "It's more of the fairies, but—"

Against her better judgment, Willow found herself walking across the lawn to get a closer look.

"They're dangerous," Dawn said, staying back by a palm tree that grew between the sidewalk and the street, more cautious after having been bitten.

"Maybe," Willow said in a soft voice. Staring as if spellbound she approached the gate that led to the backyard. "Oh, but they're so pretty, and—ooh, they're carrying something."

"A puppy." Tara walked toward the handful of glowing creatures now. "A toy poodle."

"Don't let them bite it," Dawn said.

They all watched for a moment while the handful of fairies struggled under the heavy load, working to pull it higher and higher. The poodle puppy whined and yelped.

"I think they're trying to put it on the roof," Tara said in a serene, not quite wide-awake voice.

"Oh no, we can't let them do that," Willow protested, swaying slightly as she stared at the glowing creatures. "It . . . it could fall and break a bone, or . . . or—"

The suggestion of an innocent animal in peril broke Dawn free from her paralysis. She raced across the lawn, passed Tara, jumped, and caught hold of the wriggling puppy's paw. The five fairies, unable to fight against the added weight, were forced to let go.

Dawn pulled the shivering, whimpering puppy clear of the fairies, who instantly disappeared. Tara and Willow suddenly felt more alert. Tara caught the little poodle in her arms before it could fall to the ground, but it quickly wriggled free and dashed under some bushes.

"It's okay," Willow said, trying to soothe the panicked poodle. "They're gone now." Tara knelt down and held out a hand to the puppy, but it stayed under the bushes.

"Uh, Will . . . ?" Dawn said.

The two witches turned to see that dozens of swirling fairy lights had appeared in the air above Dawn's head. Several of them pounced on her hair and yanked at it viciously. A few of them flew toward her neck and face. Dawn shrieked.

Tara and Willow ran to help her.

• • •

After finding no new signs of supernatural activity in Weatherly Park, Buffy and Xander had started to head home. They both heard the scream.

Xander cocked his head. "What was—"

"That was Dawn." Without another word, Buffy took off at a run, Xander hot on her heels. Spike must have been somewhere nearby—still spying on them, perhaps—since he appeared from the darkness and ran along with them.

"Don't need your help," Buffy said.

"I'm not doing this for you. I'm doin' it for the Little Bit."

Buffy's heart contracted as she ran, not from the exertion, but out of fear for her sister. She clenched her teeth, then stumbled at the instant jolt of pain. With lightning reflexes, Spike grabbed her arm before she could hit the pavement.

"Hey," Xander panted, catching up with them. "Watch the hands, fang-face."

"Chill, Xander. I tripped," Buffy said.

The lamplight showed her expression of determination as she set off again. As they got closer, Dawn's screams grew louder, mixed with cries for help from Tara and Willow. Now less than a block away, Buffy tried to assess the situation while running full tilt ahead. The scene was bizarre, almost surrealistic. Tara and Willow flanked Dawn protectively. Willow seemed to be trying to cast some sort of spell while Tara and Buffy's sister flailed frantically at what appeared to be a multitude of floating Christmas lights.

"Bleeding," Spike said from beside Buffy. She

didn't know if the vampire was starting to swear or simply confirming that there were injuries, but the Slayer didn't bother to ask which. She put on a burst of additional speed she didn't know she had and reached the scene seconds later. Buffy could see immediately that all the combatants were bleeding, but only in tiny trickles.

Her lightning-fast slayer reflexes switched into high gear, and Buffy began punching the twinkling lights that were in reach of her arms and kicking those that hovered lower down.

"Fairies!" Dawn gasped, prompting Buffy to wonder if her sister's injuries were worse than they seemed.

"Vampires," Tara added.

"Like fairy vamps," Willow clarified.

Spike was there in full vamp-face now. Xander arrived moments later and began flat-handing every glowing light he could see. Buffy didn't bother to count how many of the tiny assailants there were, but she knew there must be dozens of them. Without missing a beat, she kicked a glowing ball while slipping off her leather jacket, then cleared the vamps from around her sister's head and threw the jacket over it to protect her. Buffy dealt out a seemingly endless succession of precise kicks, slaps, punches, finger flicks, and full-arm swipes. Xander picked up a palm frond from the curb, where it had fallen in the recent windstorm. He swung it with broad strokes, sending several blinking lights twirling end over end with each sweep.

Tara stationed herself directly in front of Dawn

and fought the fairies one-handed, clasping Willow's hand with the other to add her powers to her friend's.

"No more onesy-twosy," Spike growled, removing his leather jacket. He twirled it in the air like a net, caught a handful of blinking lights, then hurled the coat and let go of one end in the direction of the house. The fairies shot out and struck the wall with an audible *ping, ping, ping,* then winked out. Buffy's flurry of kicks found fewer and fewer targets. She turned to check on her sister and saw a swarm of glimmering evil swirling over her head like angry hornets.

Willow made a throwing motion with one hand and said, *"Compelle escendia."* Several of the fairies flitted upward by several feet. She repeated the spell, and a few more fairies withdrew slightly.

Xander ran for the garden hose attached to a faucet at the front of the house. He turned the water on full blast and adjusted the nozzle to send out a strong spray, which he directed against any fairy that ventured close to Dawn, Tara, or Willow. Water rained down on the besieged trio. The fairies made angry buzzing sounds and scattered.

"Willow brushed water droplets from her face. We did it," she said, beaming with triumph and relief.

"I'm sensing a group hug here," Xander said, turning off the hose and wiping a hand through his damp hair.

The friends exchanged embraces and high-fives, though only a somewhat drenched Dawn hugged Spike.

Buffy at least had the good grace to apologize. "Sorry I blew you off, Spike. You were right, and . . . thanks."

Xander turned in a slow circle, looking around the recent battlefield. "So am I the only one in the dark here? What just happened?"

"We saw some little lights," Dawn explained.

"Fair folk," Tara added, shivering in her wet clothes.

"More like *un*fair folk from what I saw," Xander said. "Looked like microvamps."

"They were all glowy and kinda hypnotic. And then some tried to carry away a poodle puppy, so we had to stop them," Tara explained.

Xander stared at his childhood friend in disbelief. "So all this was to save a *poodle?*"

"I *like* poodles," Willow said in a small voice.

"But they turned into, you know, vampires," Tara said. "The fairies, I mean."

Spike, wearing a normal face again, said, "Revolting."

"I know," Willow said wistfully. "They started out so cute . . ."

"Look, I need to get Dawn home, but we all need to talk. We can do an official Scoobies run-down tomorrow morning at eight at the Magic Box. I'll call Giles and let him know," Buffy said, wondering what her Watcher would make of this development. "Fairies."

"And vampires," Dawn said.

"So, fairy vamps," Buffy concluded. "Great. Now we're in Tinkerhell."

Chapter Five

Xander had expected to spend half the night awake worrying about microvamps. But Anya had indeed treated him to dessert when he got home, and Xander had slept soundly. Sometimes it still amazed him that Anya Emerson loved *him*. Especially given the fact that she had spent more than a millennium as a vengeance demon—dedicated to punishing men for their misdeeds (real or perceived) to women.

After a quick shower in the morning, he dressed in his weekend Xander "uniform" of jeans and a plain, solid-colored tee, topped by a long-sleeved shirt. At the breakfast table, a freshly brewed cup of coffee awaited him. Anya could be obsessive compulsive in some really helpful ways. She was never late for work, she kept the apartment in excruciating order, and she took her role of supportive girlfriend as earnestly as she had taken her vengeance-demon duties. Xander sat and took a quick gulp of the steaming brown liquid. "Thanks," he said, looking across the table to where Anya sat, immersed in the morning paper.

"Did you know that the average annual temperature in Sunnydale has risen by two degrees in the last decade?" Anya said, not bothering to look up. She absently dipped a spoon into a sugar bowl on the table and dumped it into her cup of coffee.

Xander saw something move in the sugar. "Ahn."

Anya continued, oblivious to the warning tone in his voice. "You don't suppose the Hellmouth could have anything to do with global warming, do you?"

"Ahn! The sugar."

Anya looked up at him, blinked, then glanced down at the sugar bowl. She scooped up a second spoonful of sugar and tossed it into her coffee. Her eyebrows knitted momentarily in confusion at the tiny black specks traversing the rim of her coffee cup.

"Ants," Xander said.

"Oh." She flicked one away, then shrugged and stirred the rest into her coffee, put down her spoon, and took a drink.

"Okay," Xander said with a long-suffering sigh, way past being surprised at Anya's lack of alarm. He looked at the table, where several more ants were approaching the sugar bowl. Tracing their trail down a table leg, Xander found a long line of ants marching from the kitchen across the floor toward the breakfast table. He went to the kitchen, got the Windex from under the sink, and began squirting the ants.

"Why are you doing that?" Anya sounded baffled and curious.

"Because we didn't invite them. See, they're gate crashers, and I don't want them going off and telling all their little anty friends that there's a big sugar party happening at Xander and Anya's. Now is the time to step in and nip the insurgency in the bud before it gets worse. These are *ants*—that's alpha-November-tango—and if we ever see them again they are our sworn enemies."

Anya nodded earnestly, as if all this made perfect sense, and took another drink of her coffee.

"We're due at the magick shop to discuss the fairy invasion in half an hour. We need to pick up some donuts on the way," Xander said, wiping up tiny ant bodies with a kitchen towel.

"Giles likes the jelly ones," Anya said. "We need to get some. I'm planning to ask for a raise."

Xander beamed at his girlfriend. "That's my little capitalist."

Chapter Six

Buffy awoke with a splitting . . . toothache.

With a groan, she rolled over, looked at the clock, and yawned. The pain had made it difficult to fall asleep, and she had spent the night dipping in and out of a shallow slumber. When the numbers on the clock finally swam into focus, she rolled out of bed in one fluid movement and hit the decks running. Seven-thirty already.

She had a system for such "emergencies." She grabbed a brush and pulled it through her hair. By the time she reached the bathroom, she had her hair bundled into a serviceable ponytail. Fortunately, both she and Dawn had showered the night before after tending to each other's wounds from the fairy battle. So Buffy emerged from the bathroom five minutes later with her face washed and moisturized and her teeth very carefully brushed.

Back in her room she threw on some clean comfies, then she raced down the stairs. Dawn was already sitting on a stool at the island in the kitchen, finishing a breakfast of some sort of ultra-mega-sweetened puffs with milk. Her scratches and punctures from the night before stood out vividly against her pale face and neck and arms. Most likely as a gesture of defiance against her miniscule attackers, Dawn had pulled her hair into two tight braids that hung down on either side of her head.

"Does it hurt?" Buffy asked, touching her sister's cheek.

"A little," Dawn admitted. "Not much anymore." She glanced at the clock. "You slept pretty late. Can I get you an apple or anything for breakfast?"

Buffy probed her sore tooth with her tongue and found that the gums around it were now swollen. She shook her head. "Not really hungry," she said, feeling a needle-jab of guilt for lying to her sister. "Ready?"

Dawn grabbed a book bag and slung it over her shoulder. "History book, paper, everything I need right here," she reported. "Hey, want to stop at the Espresso Pump on the way to the magick shop?"

Buffy grabbed her cropped leather jacket. "You read my mind."

It was no surprise to Buffy that when she and Dawn entered the Magic Box at two minutes after eight that most of the others were already there. Tara read a book beside Willow, who had her laptop open and set up on the conference table. Anya, dressed for a regular workday, had laid out rows of boxes of merchandise on the front counter and was filling mail orders. Giles stood at one end of the counter near the table, holding a jelly donut at arm's length in his right hand, while with his left he leafed through an ancient-looking tome that lay on the counter before him.

Holding an open box of donuts, Xander approached the new arrivals. "May I offer you ladies a breakfast filled with carbohydrate goodness?"

Dawn's eyes lit up. "Dessert for breakfast. How great is that?"

Xander gave Buffy a somewhat chagrined look as Dawn selected her donut and sat at the table. Buffy eyed the donuts greedily. Soft. There was nothing there to hurt her tooth. Except the sugar, of course, and that was a risk she was willing to take. "Great, I'm famished," she said, picking up a jelly donut. She took two quick bites and washed them down with the coffee she had gotten at the Espresso Pump.

From the table, Dawn gave her an odd look. "You told me you weren't hungry."

Buffy swallowed hard. Busted. That's what she got for lying to her little sister. She shrugged it off. "That was almost half an hour ago. Now I'm starved. Thanks, Xander. Wow," she told Anya on her way over to the table, "a man who brings home a paycheck and takes care of his friends. Not a bad combination."

Anya smiled smugly. "I found him. He's mine."

Buffy took another bite of donut. "No argument here."

"Very well, let's get started then, shall we?" Giles said. "Could somebody please explain to me from the beginning just exactly what happened last night?"

"Dawn studied for her history exam," Anya said helpfully.

"Yes, yes, I was here for that," Giles said. "I meant after they left. Let's start with Buffy's patrol."

Buffy and Xander described their encounter with the Tyrloch demons, followed by their meeting Spike and him showing them the teens in Weatherly Park.

"I knew her a little—the girl, I mean," Willow said. "Cherie's father is my optometrist."

Buffy showed surprise. "The man checks your eyes once a year. And from this you got to know him well enough to meet his daughter?"

"'Proper health care is the cornerstone of success.'" Willow made a face. "The secrets of life, according to Ira Rosenberg."

Dawn, Willow, and Tara had just gotten to the part of their story where Buffy threw the jacket over Dawn's head when the shop bell jingled and a blanketed figure swept into the room. Ducking into a shady corner of the room, Spike threw off the blanket. "What'd I miss?" he asked, swatting at a few smoking patches on his arms.

"Good morning, Spike. Nothing important, really," Giles said.

"Just the recap," Buffy said. "You know: demons blah-blah-blah, *you* blah-blah-blah, dead couple blah-blah-blah, screaming blah-blah-blah, fairies blah-blah-blah, big fight. Pretty much a normal evening up until the fairies part."

"Well," Dawn said, "up until last night I didn't think that fairies really existed. I mean, I knew about vampires and things, but fairies?"

"That's because fairies are primarily European," Anya said. "Giles, do we have any more raven's beak?"

"Yes, yes, down the stairs right there," Giles said absently, and Anya went to find it.

"But these weren't just fairies," Tara pointed out.

"Nope. They were little vampires," Willow agreed. "With bumpy foreheads and fangs and everything."

"It's unnatural," Spike said in a tone of disgust.

Buffy smirked. "You're suggesting perhaps that vampires *are* natural?"

"Any rate, it doesn't make sense," Spike said. "I mean, a fairy's too small for a vampire to bite, init? And then there's the whole idea of vampires with *wings.*" He shuddered. "Like something out of a ridiculous storybook."

"Like a book of fairy tales?" Dawn asked.

"Yes, well, I must say it is odd," Giles said. He straightened some books on a shelf behind him. "Perhaps I should recategorize these," he murmured.

"C'mon, Giles, don't go all Dewey Decimal on us here. We await your words of watcherly wisdom," Xander said.

Giles looked surprised. "Indeed? That's very kind of you, Xander—and, if I might add, most alliterative. In any case, perhaps we should do what we do best."

"I take it that means it's research time?" Buffy asked.

"Quite," Giles agreed. "I suggest that Tara and Willow take a look at their books of magick whilst tutoring Dawn. Xander, Anya, and I can continue research here at the shop during business hours today. As for you, Buffy, I—"

"I've already got a plan," Buffy broke in.

"Plan Girl, that's you, Buffy. Me, I'm always Research Girl, with the books and the computer and the, you know, teachy stuff . . . ," Willow grumbled good-naturedly.

"Not to mention the problem-solving," Tara said.

"And the spells," Buffy added.

Willow sighed.

"And what about me?" Spike asked.

Giles removed his glasses. "Spike, it's daylight out. What can you do? And I'd rather not have you hanging about here with my customers."

"I could have a look about the sewers, search for any sign of the little buggers. Good place to hide from sunlight."

"Okay," Buffy said. She didn't really expect Spike to find anything, but it was a harmless assignment and would keep him out of everyone's way.

"Very well, then," Giles said. "I'd say we should get back together this evening for a debriefing."

"Great," Spike muttered. "First the sewers, then back here. How's that for a change of scenery?"

Xander rubbed his hands together. "Hey, why don't we all meet at our place instead? Say, sixish? We can do the debrief thing over Chinese."

"I'm there," Buffy said, and hurried out the door.

Anya returned from the basement holding a sealed plastic bag of beaks and a large glass jar filled with pale flakes. "I found the raven's beak. Anybody need some komodo dragon scales? We seem to be over-stocked."

Chapter Seven

Willow took her tutoring responsibilities every bit as seriously as she took her own college studies and her Scooby research duties. Tara took many things seriously. Together with Dawn, they had set up operations in the middle of the floor in Tara's dorm room.

Dawn lay on her stomach, chin propped on her fists, peering down at a history text. Willow and Tara sat side by side on the rug surrounded by stacks of books, both old and new, highlighters, pens, note cards, and Post-It pads. Color-coded place markers sprouted from the ends of most of the books.

Willow frowned down at the spiral notebook in her lap, filled with pages and pages of her neat handwriting. "Don't you find it strange that there's so little actual information available about fairies?"

Dawn's cheek dimpled. "Other than fairy tales, you mean?"

"Yes, I meant factually speaking," Willow confirmed.

"Maybe because most people don't consider the existence of fairies to be a fact," Tara said. "There's plenty about vampires."

Willow picked up another book and flipped through it. "But nothing at all about fairy vampires."

Imitating Willow, Dawn flipped through a chapter of her textbook. "Nope, not even in Jamestown." She reached for one of Willow's magick books.

Willow pulled the book away. "Stick with the history, Dawnie. You know Buffy doesn't like you to do this kind of research."

Dawn's eyes narrowed in a hostile look that was not directed toward anyone in the room. "How stupid is that?"

"Sometimes research leads to danger," Tara pointed out in a mild tone.

"Those fairies didn't look like they could turn all hurty, but they did." Willow thought back to the evening before when she had first seen the fairies, colorful glowing creatures the size of a large dragonfly, each with a tiny, very human-looking face and body. "They were like . . . like miniature angels," she murmured.

"Angels?" Tara said. She shuffled through a stack of books beside her, came up with the one she had been looking for, and flipped it open at a pale pink placeholder. "It says here that a major difference between angels and fairies—other than their wings, I mean—is that angels are celestial beings. Fairies are earth spirits, chaotic neutral."

Willow brightened. "Well, that's something at least. Good work, Tara. That could be helpful."

Dawn rolled over on her back and groaned. "Which in English means . . . ?"

"That in their natural state, fairies aren't either good or bad. They tend to do things for their own reasons, and the chaotic means that they may cause trouble of a mischievous sort."

Dawn sat up and looked at some of the scratches on her arms. "Call me picky, but I'd say that was more than mischief. Looked to me like they were trying to inflict major pain—or worse."

"Then if this book is right," Tara concluded, "those fairies can't be in their natural state. I mean, we didn't do anything to them."

"Of course not. Anyway, something is definitely wrong with this picture," Dawn said. "You know how I always imagined them?" She walked over to a shelf and picked up a heavy coffee table book that featured the art from a multitude of Disney cartoons. She opened it to a page with *Pinocchio* animation and pointed. "The Blue Fairy. That's what they should look like. Slender and blond and smiling and in a glittery blue dress." She placed the book on Willow's lap. "See?"

Willow studied the picture intently for a moment, then looked up at Tara. "She looks kind of like you."

Tara blushed and Willow leafed to a new page. "Here, this is how I always pictured fairies," she said, pointing to Tinkerbell. "Small and cute and, you know, full of spunky attitude."

"We weren't much of a Disney household," Tara said. Her face looked wistful. "No big surprise there, I guess. But the first week after I came to college, I rented *Fantasia.* I loved the fairies in that. I bought this book the next day."

Willow smiled and they shared a moment of warm silence. Willow's smile faded. "Ooh, I don't like this," she said. "As in, total yick. I don't like thinking of fairies as the bad guys. They just can't be. It's . . . it's wrong, you know?"

"I know what you mean," Tara said.

"I hate to be the voice of unreality, here, but sometimes fairies do the Bad in fairy tales," Dawn said. "Like in this one, a fairy disguises herself as an old woman by a well and asks a girl to get her a cup of water, and the girl does. As a reward the fairy casts a spell so that whenever the girl talks, gold and roses come out of her mouth."

"That doesn't sound too bad," Tara said.

"Ooh, I remember this one," Willow said. "That's not the end. The girl tells her sister, who goes down to the well. The old woman is there again, but when the old woman asks for a cup of water, the spoiled sister tells her to get it herself."

"And then"—Dawn took up the story again— "the fairy curses her. She makes it so that every time the second sister talks, coal or something else icky comes out of her mouth."

Willow nodded. "Sure. That makes sense. It was a test—simple pass/fail. The chaotic neutral fairy was just responding to the niceness, or *not-so-niceness* of the girls." She frowned again. "But we didn't do anything to provoke the fairies. Did we? They just attacked us. It just doesn't seem right. How can something that looks so cute and sweet be so . . . so . . ."

" . . . so *not?*" Dawn finished for her.

Willow bit her lower lip thoughtfully. "Right. Well, we shouldn't rush to judge. I mean, they might not be completely evil."

"What about the couple in the park?" Tara asked. "They're dead."

"I—I admit it doesn't look good, but I'd like to keep an open mind just for a little while longer. Plus, we don't really know what happened yet, or why the fairies are here. According to Anya, they're not even native to North America."

Dawn shrugged. "Yeah, there's a lot of that going around." When Willow and Tara sent her questioning glances, Dawn leaned over and flicked a finger against her history book. "According to this, neither are we."

Chapter Eight

As she had told Giles, Buffy had a plan. First stop, drugstore. In her hurry to get out the door this morning, she had stupidly ignored the pain in her tooth. "So much for a Slayer's special healing powers," she muttered to herself. She had believed she could handle the pain as long as necessary . . . and she had been wrong.

A toothache seemed like such a minor problem, a mere inconvenience, especially when compared to dead bodies in the park and heretofore mythical creatures attacking her little sister. It should have been simple to tuck the pain away at one side of her mind as she had done so often. She was the Slayer, she did what she had to do. Sure, she complained now and then just to keep Giles on his toes, but basically she took it all in stride. She had been thrown against walls, stomped on, strangled, ripped, beaten, battered, bruised, and bloodied. Not to mention killed. All in a day's work. No problem.

Except this was.

How could it possibly be that such a ridiculously small—percentage-wise speaking—part of her body could cause so much trouble? It was way past time now for a little dose of field medic self-help. She and Dawn could not afford to pay a dental bill. Buffy didn't even have a job. Unfortunately, slayage didn't come with a benefit plan. And her father was once again out of the country on some sort of business. *You're smart. You can handle this,* Buffy told herself. *And you will not worry Dawn about the whole lack-of-money thing.* If she did this right, and maybe with a little bit of luck, no one would ever suspect there had been a problem.

At the drugstore, Buffy went straight to the toothpaste aisle. She selected a high alcohol content mouthwash of the kind that promised to kill germs as soon as you unscrewed the cap. Next she got a tube of oral numbing gel, probably just an adult version of the stuff moms used on their teething babies. Next she went down the pain reliever aisle and picked up a bottle of Extra-Strength Tylenol. Last, she grabbed a box of salt from one of the food aisles and headed to the cash register to make her purchase. She waited impatiently as the chatty cashier rang up her items while talking non-stop about the mess of branches and leaves the recent storm had left in her yard, sports, the mysterious deaths of two teenagers in the park, and her plans for the weekend.

"Excuse me, do you happen to have a cup?" Buffy broke in.

The clerk never paused, but pointed to a stack of cups on top of a water cooler next to the prescription counter. Buffy paid for her purchases, thanked the clerk, and grabbed a cup on her way to the restroom at the back of the store. At the bathroom sink, she downed two Tylenol with a gulp of water. Next, she sprinkled some salt into the small cup, then filled it with warm tap water and swirled. When the salt was mostly dissolved, she swished the briny liquid through her mouth for a minute. The salt stung, and the tooth still throbbed, but Buffy knew that this was a good thing. Salt water had been her mother's cure for almost anything to do with the mouth: a sore throat, a canker sore, anything.

Buffy rinsed with the germ-killing mouthwash for good measure, then opened the tube of numbing gel and squirted a large glob onto her finger. She rubbed it on the tender areas all around the aching tooth. The inside of her mouth began to tingle. The pain didn't go away, but it faded to a more manageable level. Now she could concentrate on slaying monsters—or at least start looking for them.

Leaving the mouthwash and salt behind, Buffy tucked the Tylenol and the tube of gel into her pocket. She would start her search for the flitter vamps in Weatherly Park. Then after that, who knew? She might even check on Spike down in the sewers.

Her exploration of Weatherly Park was unsatisfying,

to say the least. She wandered on and off the trails, around trees and bushes. She looked inside the stump of a rotted-out tree that had once been struck by lightning, but found nothing to indicate that fanged fairies had been there. If the fairies truly were vampires, then they should be sleeping, or at the very least hiding, during the bright sun of day.

In a remote section of the park, beneath a low grassy hill, she found a set of steep concrete stairs leading down into the ground. Unfortunately, when she followed them down a flight into the shadows, she came up with nothing more than a dead end, a flat featureless concrete wall. Buffy had stopped being surprised about such oddities in Sunnydale.

"Weird," she said with an eyebrow shrug. "I suppose this seemed like a good idea to somebody." Maybe the city had begun a project several decades ago, a storage area or a subway system, and run out of money.

Feeling better now that the pain reliever had kicked in, Buffy bounded back up the stairs two at a time. She knew she ought to search some dark places where fairies might hide during daylight hours, but she wasn't up to being chatty with Spike in the sewers. Instead, she decided to check out a few churches in the neighborhood of the park. If that turned up nothing as well, she would broaden her search.

Chapter Nine

Because Saturday was generally the busiest sales day of the week at the Magic Box, Giles and Anya never closed down the shop except in case of direst need. As far as threats to life and limb in Sunnydale were concerned, vampire fairies hardly qualified.

A statuesque woman, six feet tall if she was an inch, entered the store and began to shop. The dark-haired Amazon wore half a dozen rings, an amber necklace, a swirling, multicolored skirt, and a broad smile.

"Good morning, Miss Ray," Anya greeted her. "May I offer you a soothing herbal tea? Please feel free to make copious purchases." She leaned down and whispered to Xander, "Deb is one of our regulars. It's always a good omen when she comes. She pays cash. We make lots of money."

"Thank you, darlin'. I'd love some tea," the customer drawled. "Did my order come in?"

Anya nodded. "The Pokémon tarot deck? They're already behind the counter for you. And, if I might suggest, some komodo dragon scales and a package of bogweed incense would make a fine accompaniment." Miss Ray looked intrigued.

Comfortably seated at the table with his feet up on another chair, Xander watched the comings and goings in the shop with distant interest. He had chosen three of the most likely looking candidates from Giles's collection of books on magickal creatures. They lay open on the table in front of him. Anya, as usual, staffed the checkout counter, and Giles roamed about the store helping customers find what they needed. "Don't you think it's the least bit strange," Xander said during a lull in the store traffic, "that even the Giles International Library of the Weird contains almost no facts about fairies?"

Anya straightened some items on a shelf behind the counter. "Not really. Most of the time they don't want to be seen." Several more customers jingled into the store and began browsing.

"Of course, there was that account of multiple fairy sightings back in 1917 in England." Giles picked up a newish-looking book and flipped it open. "Ah, here it is: the case of the Cottingley fairies. A couple of schoolgirls claimed to have seen fairies in the woods. Took photographs and everything."

"Fairies prefer forest habitats," Anya said. She

pointed Miss Ray toward a tabletop fountain fashioned from amethyst crystals.

"There were real pictures?" Xander asked. "The point-shoot-and-develop kind?"

Giles raised his eyebrows and nodded. "Well, good enough to fool Sir Arthur Conan Doyle, at any rate. He wrote an article about the fairies that appeared in *The Strand* in 1920. Of course, the whole thing was later proven to be a hoax. Much, much later when the two girls had both become grandmothers, they finally admitted they had made the whole thing up."

"Yes," Anya said with a smug smile, "at least that's what they said later."

"Hey, wasn't there a movie about this?" Xander asked. "I mean, not that I ever saw the film—it being about fairies and all—but I remember hearing about it."

Giles took off his glasses and rubbed his eyes. "Yes, I believe it was called *Fairy Tale: A True Story*, or something to that effect. At any rate, it's not applicable to our present situation."

"No fangs?" Xander asked.

"Quite." Giles picked up a slip of paper from the counter next to him and placed it like a bookmark into the book he was holding. Then, as if just noticing what it was, he scowled, folded it carefully, and tucked it into his shirt pocket. Anya helped a customer who came into the shop just then, and Xander went back to reading, but when he looked up half an hour later, Giles had not moved and was staring distractedly out the window through its curtain of hanging beads.

"Hey, here's a few tasty tidbits," Xander said.

"Do you have a gift box for these dehydrated frogs?" a slender, balding man with bright eyes asked Anya.

"Of course," she said brightly. Then to Xander, "Go ahead. We're listening." She bent down and rummaged behind the counter.

"According to this," Xander said, "fairies either live all by themselves—that's a solitary fairy—or in large clusters called troops. This could just be my army instincts talking here, but I'd say we're dealing with the troop variety. Big duh on that one, huh?" He glanced back down at the page. "Apparently fairies are matriarchal, and each troop is led by a queen. Of course in the army, our troops weren't led by a queen." He gave a sheepish grin. "At least, not that I can remember." He looked at Giles, waiting for a reaction.

"Yes, yes, that's all very interesting, I'm sure," the Watcher said absently, tapping a finger against his lips.

Anya stood up with the gift box in her hand and wrapped the bright-eyed man's dehydrated frogs.

Xander shook his head. "Anyone else? Yo, Tweed Man, something wrong?"

The bell tinkled as the satisfied customer left the shop. Anya leaned across the counter toward Xander. "Giles got a parking ticket," she said in a conspiratorial voice.

"Whoa! Takin' a drive on the wild side, eh, Giles?"

"It wasn't a speeding ticket, Xander. It was a parking ticket—and completely undeserved, I might add."

"He's decided not to pay the ticket," Anya said,

sorting through and bagging a substantial pile of Miss Ray's purchases.

Xander gave a silent whistle of surprise. "Civil disobedience. Why, Giles, this is a side of you I've never seen before." Like an eager child waiting for a story, Xander scrambled on top of the conference table and sat with his legs crossed, facing the Watcher. "Hold the presses. This is way bigger news than vampire fairies. So tell the truth, Giles. Did you do it? Did you park in a no-parking zone?"

"Yes. I mean, no. I mean, that is to say . . ." Giles glared at him in exasperation. "That area across the street has always been a perfectly legal parking place, but last week somebody at city hall decided it was time to lower the curb to make it more friendly for prams and wheelchair users. Apparently someone put up a temporary no-parking sign, but it was completely obscured by a tree branch."

Xander put his elbows on his knees and leaned forward. "How much is the ticket?"

"Eighteen dollars. But that's not the point, is it? It was a completely innocent mistake."

Xander's eyes narrowed. "Ah, a completely innocent man on the run from the law. It's a classic."

Giles sighed, removed his glasses, and glared at Xander again. "I am not, as you say, on the run from the law. I've decided not to pay the ticket because I am due to argue my case in court on Monday afternoon."

Xander gave him a disbelieving look. "You're going to court for eighteen dollars? That's barely two pizzas."

"Thank you," Anya said, loading Miss Ray's arms with bags and boxes. "Please return as soon as possible to make further purchases."

"It's the principle of the thing, isn't it?" Giles said defensively to Xander.

Xander looked thoughtful. "I guess. Plus, there's the two pizzas. . . ."

With a clinking of the bell, a new customer entered the shop. Giles glanced pointedly from Xander, to the conference table on which he sat, and back to Xander.

Xander scrambled down and took his seat again. "Well, good luck Monday. We'll all be rootin' for you."

Giles slid his glasses back onto his face and browsed the page that was open in front of him. "Thank you," he said absently. "Now, have you found anything about fairies?"

Chapter Ten

Spike, a.k.a. William the Bloody, was no stranger to the sewers of Sunnydale. In fact, he was no stranger to sewers in general. In almost any city, they were one of the safest ways for a vampire to get around during the day. Although he had a keenly honed sense of smell, he could avoid the stench altogether when necessary by choosing not to breathe. Today in the sewers? Definitely necessary.

His eyes were naturally dark-adjusted, so he could see as well here in the sewers as humans could see in bright daylight. Of course, not all of the tunnels were completely dark. In the upper levels emergency lights attached to the rounded walls trickled dim light onto the sewer floor at regular intervals. Occasional patches of sunlight, mostly indirect, filtered down from storm drains, gratings, or manhole covers overhead to highlight the roots, leaves, and pools of standing water (or worse substances) that lent the brick and concrete passages such a festive air.

As sewers went, this area wasn't bad. Fat metal pipes ran along the wide corridors, and there was only enough liquid on the floor to come halfway up Spike's shoes. All in all, it was nearly as cozy as Spike's very own crypt. He would, of course, need to clean his shoes after his explorations. Spike was a fastidious vampire and had an image to maintain after all—an image that up until recently had included slaying slayers, not befriending them or offering to help them with their dirty work. Certainly not falling in love with one.

His mouth twisted into an expression of self-ridicule. Ah, how the mighty had fallen. He supposed he could always blame it on the chip the Initiative had installed in his head. The chip did not allow him to harm humans in any way without bringing torrents of pain gushing through his head.

From the corner of one eye, Spike saw a glowing flash toward one side of the tunnel. He walked over and crouched beside it, tweaking the long tails of his leather coat, so that they didn't drag in the muck. The glow emanated from nothing more exciting than a child's tennis shoe with a flashing light embedded in the sole. He glanced around. No bones. No child. No second shoe. It must have washed down into the sewer through one of the storm drains in the curbs that lined the street above.

Strange thing to find in the sewer, Spike thought,

continuing along the conduit. But then, he had often found strange things in sewers. A few years back he had seen a spider monkey in a New York City sewer. Then there was the time he had been walking through the sewers in Paris with Dru. There they had found a raised, abandoned chamber that, upon investigation, proved to be stocked with piles of hand-written sheet music, sheaves of blank paper, writing implements, a small cache of musical instruments, bits of candles, a flint to light them with, some straw, and a ragged blanket. Spike had often wondered if someone else had also found this room and related the tale to Gaston Leroux, who had turned it into his novel, *The Phantom of the Opera.*

Spike nudged his foot against a half-submerged striped container, which turned out to be an empty bucket that had once held fried chicken. He realized that he was starting to feel a bit peckish. Maybe there would be time to stop for a shot of O-neg later this evening. Spike moved on.

Perhaps his favorite unusual object he had encountered in his sewery sojourns was an entire horse-drawn hansom cab, minus the horse, with a nobleman unconscious on the passenger seat. How or why the entire carriage had gotten down into the London sewers was anyone's guess, but Dru, Darla, Angel, and Spike—never ones to refuse an unexpected gift—had shared the teatime snack.

Those had been the days.

Spike came to the juncture of two sewer tunnels and turned left. Up ahead he saw what appeared to be a heap of dark rags and quickened his footsteps toward it. When he was a few feet away, he took a cautious breath and smelled sewage . . . mixed with blood. Spike bent over the ragged pile and pushed some of the cloth aside to reveal an unnaturally pale face. He searched for a pulse in the man's neck and found none. His fingers came away wet; he smelled, then licked them. The blood was still fresh. Strangely, the man's face was not contorted in agony. The smattering of dark stubble along the man's gaunt jaw line framed an almost beatific smile, as if the man were having a pleasant dream.

Spike pulled back another layer of rags and saw that the man wore army fatigues that appeared to have been "fatigued" for at least a decade now. A name patch above the breast pocket said Hoyt. *A down-on-his-luck vet?* Spike wondered. *Or merely a homeless man with a preference for durable clothing?* After a quick assessment of the man's temples, neck, and wrists, Spike was forced to conclude by the tiny puncture marks there that this was again the work of microvamps. Within the past couple of hours, no less. Daytime. Though in the sewers the time of day hardly mattered.

Something twinkled at the periphery of his vision. An oddly bright aqua color. He knew instantly what it must be. In a split second Spike was on his feet and in pursuit.

The aqua light flashed and bobbed around a corner. Spike ran full tilt after it. Through one tunnel, down a level, to another passageway. So it went, with the aqua light always just out of reach.

Spike jumped onto a shelf where two uneven tunnels connected to each other. Back up a level. The glow was farther ahead now. Rounding yet another corner, Spike increased his speed—only to slip and fall in a puddle of rank-smelling semiliquid goo. Covered with brownish slime, he looked up just in time to see the aqua glimmer disappear into a grating in the sewer wall.

Buffy's search of the basements, catacombs, and rec rooms beneath the churches of Sunnydale proved fruitless. She kept her toothache under tight control with the Tylenol and the numbing gel, but boredom and discouragement seemed to amplify her pain.

She was eyeing the holy water thoughtfully in a small Catholic church when a priest approached her from the direction of the altar. "May I be of help to you, child?" he said in a lilting Irish accent.

Buffy glanced at the floor, decided that honesty would be the best policy, then looked back at the priest. "To tell the truth, I could use some more holy water."

"I suppose that could be arranged, dependin' on why you'll be needin' it," he said, an amused expression in his dark eyes. "And would there be anythin' else I could do today to help?"

Buffy sighed and lifted a corner of her mouth in a yeah-right expression. "Not unless you know an awful lot about fairies."

The short priest's eyebrows went up. "The wee ones? The Irish have a long history with the Fair Folk." He glanced around the church. "But perhaps we'd best talk about this in my office."

Buffy looked at the priest in a new light now: a resource. *Bingo.*

Chapter Eleven

Xander and Anya picked up Chinese takeout and walked back to their apartment. Xander clutched several white bags to his chest with both arms. Anya swung a handled plastic bag filled with napkins, hot red peppers, chopsticks, packets of soy sauce and hot Chinese mustard, and fortune cookies. Every block or so she reached into the bag, pulled out a few peppers, popped them whole into her mouth, and chewed.

"I hope our friends won't find fault with our housekeeping. We are working people, after all, and there was no time for extra cleaning. Perhaps if we serve an alcoholic beverage their judgment will be impaired and they won't notice any messes."

"It'll be fine, Ahn," Xander assured her. "The apartment always looks perfect. If there's one thing we do really well, it's keep our apartment neat."

Because Xander was carrying most of the Chinese food, Anya opened the door to the apartment for him. He went over to the kitchen counter and started to put down his bags.

"Xander, no. Not there," Anya practically yelled. "Over on the table."

He turned and carried the bags to the table instead. "All right, hearing still works perfectly. No need to yell. See, everything's right on the table where you want—"

"You are no longer welcome in my home," Anya said. Her voice was filled with cold fury.

"Ahn, I . . . it was just a . . . misunder—"

Before Xander knew what was happening, Anya had crossed to their tool drawer, opened it, snatched out a hammer, and swung it down hard—onto the kitchen counter. "You've been warned," Anya said. "Now—you—will—pay—the—price." She punctuated each word with a bang of the hammer.

Xander hurried over to her and grabbed her wrist. He looked down at the counter which she had been hammering and noticed for the first time black rivers of ants flowing across it. Several ants were carrying crumbs of toast or cheese puffs that seemed to be an order of magnitude larger than the ants themselves.

"Whoa, whoa, whoa there, slugger," he said. "At first you think they're harmless, now you're ready to declare World War Three on them? Let's pretend for a moment that we're reasonable people. Put the hammer down."

Anya looked at him, her eyes wide, their expression not quite rational. "Xander, we have guests arriving in less than half an hour."

They had been together long enough that Xander knew full well when to switch tactics. "All right, I'm with you. These are insurgents, parasitic rebels. They deserve to be nuked. The counterinsurgency begins forthwith. But just remember, if we damage anything in the apartment we'll have to *pay* for it."

Anya's expression changed to one of outright horror. Xander let go of her wrist. "Pay—our money?" She let the hammer fall from her hand to the floor and anxiously examined the countertop for signs of permanent damage, then swung open a cupboard, snatched a cookbook and slammed it down flat on thousands of hapless ants. "Pay?" she repeated, slamming the book down again. "I didn't ask them here. How could anyone hold me responsible?" She glared at Xander. "I won't let them take my money. Who is responsible?" she demanded.

Xander thought for a moment. "Well, whoever owns the building, I suppose. That's why God made landlords and managers, I guess. Yup, that's it." He grabbed the phone, glanced down at the list of numbers taped next to it, and dialed.

Minutes later the apartment manager, an ample redhead in her early fifties, was at their door. "Here," she said, handing Xander a container of Anti-Gone, an aerosol can with a picture of an ant weeping at a gravesite on it.

"That's *it?*" Xander asked. "Bug spray?"

The manager rolled her brown eyes. "They're ants, not a pack of rabid dogs. That ought to do it." She made an indifferent gesture with one hand. "If not, call me."

Xander went back to the kitchen, where Anya was wiping up legions of dead anty bodies. He chuckled and made a sound like an air-raid siren, then knelt by the baseboards. "This is not a drill, boys. You are going down." He began to spray.

Chapter Twelve

"Is anybody else starting to think our Scooby gang is obsessed with food?" Buffy asked, staring doubtfully down into a carton of kung-pao chicken.

Xander pressed his lips together and pushed them out in a considering look. "What'd you have for lunch?"

Buffy grimaced. "I, uh, got busy. Guess I just forgot." She couldn't very well admit that her tooth had been paining her too much to eat anything.

Xander nodded. "Willow?"

"Chips," Tara answered for her friend.

Then, seeing Buffy's surprised look, Willow added, "Oh, but Sun Chips. So, very nutritious."

"And orange juice," Dawn said.

Xander was grinning by now. "Giles, Anya?" he asked the last two people in the room.

"We, uh, had some apples between customers," Giles said.

Xander leaned back in his chair at the dinette table and spread his arms in a see-what-I-mean gesture. "Hardly what I'd call obsession. Besides, they say an army marches on its stomach. We eat to keep up our strength. No one's going to be caught unprepared." He crossed his arms over his chest. "Not on my watch."

Buffy decided that her tooth probably couldn't handle the peanuts and celery in the kung-pao chicken, so she opted for the chicken chow mein instead.

"I believe we have significantly more important matters to discuss than how often one needs to eat," Giles said.

Dawn tilted her head to one side. "I wonder how often vampire fairies need to eat."

"Mmm. Indeed." Giles helped himself to some fried rice. "Yes, well, perhaps I'd better go first. Get the ball rolling so to speak about what we've learned today." He raised a loose fist to his mouth in a thoughtful pose for a moment, then cleared his throat in that ahem-the-lecture-is-about-to-start sort of way. "Countless cultures around the world have mythology that scholars prefer to interpret as references to fairies— such as pixies or genies. Thomas Keightley, for example, believed the derivation to come from the Persian word *peri,* later bastardized by the Arabians to *feri,* but it's clear, at least for our purposes, that the linguistic origin is of less importance than are the few factual references to these creatures."

"Did you try the Watcher Diaries?" Buffy asked.

Giles nodded. "Nothing, I'm afraid. There is a dearth of factual accounts, but I pieced together what I could from my collections of reference books. As best I could ascertain, fairies themselves actually originated in mainland Europe."

"In Italy," Anya added.

Giles blinked several times. "Yes, quite. They were known as the *fatae* amongst their own kind. It is believed that the word *fatae* derived from the Latin *Fata,* the goddess of fate. It would seem that fairies tend to be rather gregarious."

Xander spoke up now. "Sure, you'll find the occasional lean and hard-bitten loner fairy, but for the most part they like to live in merry little bands of teeny-weeny boy fairies and itsy-bitsy girl fairies, all ruled by an eensy-weensy lady fairy."

"These bands," Giles continued smoothly, "are known as *fatara,* or troops. Each troop is ruled by a queen."

Buffy poured herself some juice from a pitcher on the table. "You mean like some kind of überfairy?"

"I suppose so, yes." Giles pulled apart a pair of disposable chopsticks. "From Italy, the *fatae* migrated to France, where the name was shortened and they became known as the *feie.*"

"May I offer anyone deep-fried pig in fluorescent orange gravy?" Anya asked brightly.

"Sweet-and-sour pork anyone?" Xander translated.

Giles accepted the carton. "Unfortunately, true scholarship on the subject seems to be somewhat spotty at best. We do know that fairies—or at least stories of fairies—had reached the British Isles by the fifteen hundreds. Spenser's *The Faerie Queene* was published in 1590, and the Scribe himself included a story of Fairy Queen Mab in *Romeo and Juliet* in 1595."

"Ooh, Mercutio's speech. I memorized it for Miss Miller's class junior year," Willow said. She recited in a dramatic tone,

> *"And in this state she gallops night by night*
> *Through lovers' brains, and then they*
> *dream of love;*
> *O'er courtiers' knees, that dream on*
> *court'sies straight;*
> *O'er lawyers' fingers, who straight dream*
> *on fees;*
> *O'er ladies' lips, who straight on kisses*
> *dream—"*

"Yes, excellent. Thank you, Willow. And what did your studies turn up?" Giles asked. "Er, do we have any mu shu?"

"Yes, and I ordered extra pancakes." Anya passed him the carton, the pancakes, and the plum sauce.

"Well, kinda good news, bad news," Willow said, answering Giles's first question. "The good news is that there are hundreds of sites on the internet dedicated to fairies. Thousands, maybe."

"And the bad?" Giles asked.

Willow pointed her chopsticks at him. "Giles, it's *the Web.* Most of these people aren't academics presenting their research. They're hobbyists, figurine collectors, fiction writers, high-school students, and who knows what else. Sure, maybe there's a few nuggets of data hiding here and there, but do you know how hard it is to sift through all the . . . the *junk* to find anything that's actually useful? How do I decide whether a source is reputable or not? I mean, we're talking fairies, here. You said it yourself: There aren't a lot of verifiable facts available." She lowered her chopsticks and took a bite of rice. "We did find out that fairies have a weak sort of woo-woo mesmerizing power called glamour. That may be how they keep their victims from fighting or running away. We felt a bit of the glamour last night. If you're not aware of it and you stare at them too long, you can get sort of sucked in, I guess. Oh, ick—not sucked. Forget the sucked."

Handing Willow a spring roll, Tara picked up the narrative. "And we're pretty sure they're chaotic neutral—a fact that's also supported by quite a few fairy tales. It's one of several themes that come up over and over again. Dawn had a good observation about that."

Dawn grimaced as everybody's eyes turned toward her. "It wasn't that big a deal. They wouldn't let me do any real research. There are some simple things in fairy tales, though. Like fairies—duh—have magick." She crunched down on a crispy deep-fried wonton. "Also, they're usually cute or beautiful, and they generally return a good deed for a good deed and a bad deed for a bad one."

"Kind of like a Fairy Golden Rule," Xander mused.

"Yes, I suppose it is. Fair enough," Giles said. "We should take that into account. Buffy, did you find out anything that might be of any use?"

Buffy swallowed a mouthful of chow-mein noodles and drew a deep breath. "Well, first I did a totally useless sweep of Weatherly Park. I thought I might have found something. There's this little grassy hill in the park. Some stairs lead down into it. But I went down the stairs and . . . big blank wall."

"A stairway to nowhere?" Xander considered this, wiping a drop of sweet-and-sour sauce from his chin with a napkin. "Sounds mighty suspicious. You sure?"

"Nothing but a bunch of concrete," Buffy confirmed.

Willow seemed to brighten. "I could look at the city plans for you and find out what it was. That should be way easier than getting information about fairies."

Buffy smiled. "Thanks, Will. Anyhow, post-park I decided to visit some of the churches. A lot of them have, you know, dark undergroundy-type places where fairy-sized vampires might try to hide during the day."

"And did you find any?" Dawn asked.

Buffy made a face. "None. Oh, but I did meet Father Murphy. He's Irish. I mean *real* Irish, like 'top o' the mornin' and 'where's my shillelagh' and all that. He says there are real fairies in Ireland, and that lots of people there believe in them. But they worship this, like, old religion and they would never, *ever* come near a church."

Anya made a *pfft* sound. "I could have told you that."

Just then, a knock sounded at the door and Anya went to answer it.

"Spike, *avanti,*" she said, opening the door to him.

He swept into the room, answering her in Italian. "*Grazie. Ho molto fame.*"

"We're eating already," Anya said. "You're very late."

The blond vamp held up a bottle made of dark glass. "Yeah, well I kind of figured it was B.Y.O.B." When she gave him a blank look, he raised his eyebrows. "Bring your own blood? Picked up some Chateau de Piggy." He walked over to the table. "Had to stop by the ol' crypt anyway, clean myself up a bit. Didn't think you all would appreciate the way I smelled after exploring the sewers."

Xander gave the vampire a sarcastic smile. "And yet, no real improvement in smell."

Spike ignored the jibe. "Say, is that hot-and-sour soup?"

"*Si accomodi, prego,*" Giles said. "And help yourself. We were just lamenting the fact that we have no real first-hand sources of knowledge about fairies."

Anya blinked. "Of course we do."

Buffy probed her sore tooth with her tongue and said, "I'm not sure we can really count Father Murphy. He's never seen any fairies in person."

Anya gave her a condescending look. "I'm not talking about Father Murphy. I meant me."

Chapter Thirteen

Ordinary fairies were, at best, capricious creatures. Of course, Mabyana and her troop were not ordinary garden-variety fairies. And they were certainly not at their best. In the centuries since The Change, they had come to understand their vampire nature, combining it with their fairy personalities and abilities. Becoming vampire fairies had not necessarily been a good thing, but it could be fun. An edge of malice had added itself to their mischievous merrymaking. But the fairies never let that new element ruin their good time.

Tonight, the golden Fairy Queen and her followers planned to "do the town" of Sunnydale—literally.

Dorse, dumb as a rock, started off the games with his favorite witty prank. His aqua hair glowed as the fairies, by twos and threes, flitted from door to door on a quiet street, ringing doorbells and tapping at windows.

In each case, they quickly darted to a safe distance from which they could enjoy the looks of confusion or worry on the faces of the residents who answered their doors.

Within fifteen minutes, no fewer than three police cars had arrived to check out reports of burglars, stalkers, and peeping toms. Dorse, along with the rest of the fairies who had come out to enjoy the evening's revels, twinkled with laughter and spun somersaults in the air. Queen Mabyana laughed with them, but decided it was now time to let someone else lead the charge. She gave Tressa that honor.

"Let's remember to be creative," Mab said. "The Fair Ones have standards to uphold."

Always a nature-lover at heart, Tressa already had a target in mind. Hair the color of ripe apricots streamed out behind the girl fairy as she made a bee-line for the flowers. The Sunnydale Botanical Society had earned a reputation for cultivating one of the finest rose gardens in all of Southern California. Every year the gardens attracted thousands of visitors to Sunny-dale, and tonight Tressa was one of them.

At the very first bush, she stopped to hover in front of a bright yellow blossom and inhale its scent. Then, impulsively, she spread her arms wide, flitted forward, and embraced the flower. Within seconds, as if shown on a stop-motion camera, the bloom withered and died. But Tressa did not let go. Bit by bit, the stem began to wilt, then the leaves, death spreading throughout the bush and down to the roots. Only after it was completely shriveled did Tressa flutter above the bush, survey her handiwork, and turn a delighted pirouette. Her sheer teal dress swirled around her. "*Perfect.*"

Mabyana, getting into the spirit, chose a rose bush for herself and threw her arms around a delicate rosebud. All about the garden, Vesuva, Dorse, Steet, and the others selected rose bushes . . . and rotted them from the inside out.

When every bush had been drained of life, Mab allowed Lucket to have his turn. The silver-haired fairy, who always wore lavender tights and a lavender jerkin, decided that family pets, especially outdoor dogs and cats, would be his special focus tonight. Under his direction, the troop harried every animal they could find, poking, tweaking, and nibbling until cats took refuge in trees or under houses, and dogs fled from their homes or barked until their masters came to shush them. For good measure, Lucket picked up Frisbees, kites, and other lightweight toys and deposited them on rooftops.

Next, Vesuva took her turn. Followed by a swarm of fairies, the raven-haired sprite skimmed along the surfaces of dozens of swimming pools and reflecting ponds. In each one she touched, the water turned a garish and unnatural color: day-glow orange, chartreuse, fuchsia. The colored water, in addition to making the neighborhoods look like a child's paint box when viewed from above, had delightful staining properties. In fact, any human or animal that bathed in those pools would emerge looking like a dyed Easter egg.

Steet, of the cherry red, punk-cut hair, chose the streetlamps. Each narrow whipped-cream-dollop lamp rested atop a tapered column. Steet landed on the first one and concentrated on the light until it shattered in a burst of broken glass and sparks. Twinkling their amusement, the rest of the troop joined in.

Mab smiled in satisfaction. So much fun, and the night was still young.

Chapter Fourteen

Everyone stared at Anya. Buffy choked and spluttered.

"Bloody 'ell," Spike said.

Xander shook his head as if to clear it. "Is it just me, or does anybody else think it's just a little bit late to be bringing this up?"

Giles took off his glasses and cleaned them. "Anya, you do realize that we've all spent the past ten hours trying to find out more about fairies?"

Anya's smile was cheery. "Oh, yes."

"And yet you felt no particular compulsion to share this fact with us?"

Anya looked confused. "Well, I wasn't hiding it. I told you that fairies don't like to be seen and that they prefer to live in forests."

Giles put his glasses back on. "Well, I suppose I'd

just assumed that you'd gotten that information through research."

Anya shrugged. "You never asked for more information, so I figured it wasn't that important. And you were worried about your traffic ticket—"

"Giles, you got a ticket?" Buffy said, looking at her mentor with shock.

"Easy there, Sheriff Buffy, it's just a parking thing," Xander said. Buffy looked at Giles for confirmation.

"I'm innocent," Giles said.

"—and Xander was doing research and I was helping the customers," Anya continued as if she had never been interrupted. "I figured if you wanted to know more, you would ask."

"I think we'd all like to hear what you know about fairies," Tara said with a smile of encouragement.

"Yeah, and *how* do you know?" Dawn asked. "Did you see them?"

Looking pleased at their sudden interest, Anya began to talk. "In the past thousand years, I've only seen fairies three times."

"So, I take it this was all part of a vengeance-demon gig, then?" Xander asked.

Anya smiled proudly at him. "Yes. The first time was at a christening ceremony." Anya made a face. "The father had been unfaithful to the mother while she was pregnant, so I was there in my usual capacity. And since the mother had called me to take vengeance, she invited fairies to the christening ceremony." She looked around at the rapt listeners. "Fairies give the best gifts, you know—when people are kind to them. At least they used to. The second time was on midsummer's eve. I had been following a man who was having a tryst with his wife's cousin and there they were dancing in the glen—the fairies, I mean. Not the man and the cousin."

She made a dismissive gesture. "I only saw them for a minute. But the last time was in sixteenth-century Italy. A powerful sorceress named Devara called on me to take vengeance on her fiancé, who had disappeared. I can tell you she was madly in love with him, but after he was missing for a week Devara suspected the worst: infidelity. So I went after her fiancé to find out what happened." She sighed. "It turned out that some mischievous fairies had led him astray in the forest."

"Oh, well, that doesn't sound too serious," Willow said.

"It is if Sabina—a notorious and lusty female vampire—just happens to be hiding out in that forest," Anya said.

"Way serious," Buffy agreed.

"So . . . then what?" Dawn said. "You found the body?"

"Worse," Anya said. Dawn frowned in confusion.

"He was a vampire, Little Bit," Spike said. "Sabina sired him."

Dawn's mouth formed into a little O, and she fell silent.

Buffy took a deep breath. "So what happened when you broke the news to the sorceress?"

"She didn't take it well," Anya said. "Devara made

herself a stake from a broomstick and set off into the forest to find her fiancé and Sabina. I went along—strictly for moral support, since I was duty-bound to help her. You see, technically, her fiancé *had* strayed, though he really didn't have much choice about it. When we found Sabina, the fairies were hovering overhead just to see what would happen. The sorceress fought Sabina and staked her without mercy. But for some reason Devara's fiancé didn't put up a fight, and she couldn't bring herself to kill him. Together we worked a spell, an old magic that goes back almost to the dawn of time. As powerful as we were, it almost killed both of us. We shattered the vampire demon into a thousand pieces and drove it from her fiancé's body."

Dawn had a small, hopeful smile. "So he was saved, then?"

"No, Dawnie. He was dead," Buffy said gently.

"I didn't realize what she was going to do until it was too late," Anya went on. "The sorceress was so angry with the fairies for leading her fiancé into danger that she sent the shattered demon spirit into the troop of fairies."

"You can do that?" Xander asked.

"I can't," Anya replied, "but she did. Then she took her fiancé home, mourned him, and buried him.

Buffy gave a sour smile. "And they all lived happily ever after."

"So," Giles said at last, "these vampire fairies are most likely the same troop of fairies you met in that forest in Italy."

"Probably," Anya agreed with a confident smile.

"Ahn," Xander said, "aren't you at all afraid that they're here for, you know, revenge?"

"On whom?" she asked. Her wide-eyed gaze was completely serious.

"You?" he said. "You know, Doctor Frankenstein's right-hand demon? You made it possible for the sorceress to curse those fairies."

"Oh," Anya said, looking surprised. "I suppose. But only in the most literal sense. And anyway, fairies are migratory. It could just be a coincidence that they're here in Sunnydale. After all, it has been five hundred years."

"Am I alone in this, or does anyone else think it's some sort of *colossal* coincidence that these things just happened to show up in the same town where Anya lives?" Xander asked.

"Sure, if you call demons showing up in Sunnydale a coincidence," Buffy said. "Xander, if they migrated here, maybe they were drawn by the Hellmouth. Happens to vamps all the time."

Xander brought out a box of toothpicks from the kitchen and started chewing on one while Anya passed out fortune cookies.

Dawn broke her cookie open and pulled out the narrow strip of white paper from inside. "'Fortune smiles on the diligent,'" she read. Dawn rolled her eyes. "Do you think they get frustrated teachers to write these things?"

"Or parents, maybe," Willow said. She shared hers

next. "'Your greatest strength may be your greatest weakness.'"

Xander gave a sage nod. "Ambiguity. Always a fine choice in fortune telling. Mine says, 'Conformity is the refuge of the undeveloped personality.' I think I've got that one under control. What about yours, Ahn?"

"It's very strange." Anya frowned. "It says 'A gift from the heart carries no price tag.' That doesn't make any sense, does it?"

"In a way," Tara said. "About as much sense as mine makes. 'A kind word now may save a harsh word later.' I'm not so much of a harsh-word person, anyway."

Spike made a face. "Better advice than 'Remain alert to the feelings of those around you.'" He glanced curiously at Buffy.

"'Deal honestly with your friends and justly with your enemies,'" Buffy read. "No arcane meanings there—although *I'm* starting to wonder if maybe these are written by watchers with too much time on their hands." Buffy bit down on her fortune cookie and instantly regretted it. Pain rocked her back in her seat and she dropped the unfinished portion of cookie onto the table.

Xander scooped it up and stuffed it into his mouth. "Waste not," he chided.

Giles opened his fortune cookie and read, "'Change lies just around the corner.'" He looked serious and introspective.

"Here, save yourself a trip." Xander fished briefly in his pocket and plunked a few coins on the table in front of Giles with a grin. "Change is everywhere."

Dawn's hand hit the table with a loud slap. Everyone looked at her in surprise. She turned her hand over and looked at it. "Eew—ants! They were trying to get into the hot-and-sour soup."

Anya stood, a look of alarm registering on her face. Xander scrambled into the kitchen for glass cleaner and towels. Everyone moved leftover Chinese food out of harm's way while Xander and Anya squirted and wiped. "That's the third time," Xander said.

"Really?" Willow asked. "Hey, I could try a toned-down version of a teleportation spell if you want me to. I've been practicing."

"Willow," Tara said with a look of deep concern in her eyes. "You shouldn't be using magick to solve simple everyday problems. It's not right."

Willow looked a bit disappointed. "It was just a suggestion. No big. We don't have to."

Xander grabbed the phone and started dialing. After a short and slightly heated conversation, he turned back to his friends. "They're sending out an exterminator tomorrow morning."

"Tomorrow?" Buffy said. "On a Sunday?"

"All preliminary attempts at negotiation with the hostiles failed. No more Mister Nice Guy." Xander shrugged. "The manager said she would arrange it." He clapped his hands and rubbed them together. "Okay, what do we do about these microvamps? You think we could get Herbie the elf to pull out all their teeth?"

Willow seemed to consider this seriously. "Not unless they were much bigger."

Xander sighed. "Can you say, 'Honey, I shrunk the vamps'?"

Chapter Fifteen

After dodging into Xander and Anya's bathroom to reapply numbing gel to her tooth, Buffy was ready for a war counsel. Muttering something about a headache, she also downed two Tylenol. Spike caught her eye and she could tell that he didn't believe her excuse for a moment. He knew her tooth was still bothering her.

Before Spike could make a comment that might give her away, Buffy said, "So what's the plan?"

"But—," Spike began.

"Well, the usual, I suppose," Giles said. "I mean, it's vampires, isn't it?"

Spike cleared his throat. "I have—"

Willow yanked at a strand of her red hair. "Oh, but they're fairies too. Maybe they're not totally full of vile evilness like, you know, human vampires." She glanced over at Spike. "Present company, uh, excepted—kind of."

Spike looked affronted. "What's a bloke got to—"

Tara frowned. "But they killed those two high-school students in the park, so we know they're dangerous."

Spike spread his hands as if to say, *I told you so*. "That's what I've been—"

"Well, on the bright side, no new bodies," Dawn said.

With an impatient growl, Spike stood, climbed onto his chair. "Hello? Talking here."

"Whoa, there, Albino Boy—and by that I mean no disrespect to melanin-deprived Americans," Xander said. "What's got your dander up?"

Spike stepped down from the chair, twirled it around, and sat facing the table on the backward chair with his arms resting on the seat back. "I spent the entire day slogging through bloody sewer tunnels and nobody even bothers to ask me?"

"Aww," Buffy said with mock sympathy. "How was work? Rough day at the office?" In all honesty she had, in the aftermath of Anya's shocking revelations, forgotten to ask the blond vamp what he might have found. Besides, she had never expected his day to be any more successful than hers had been, though, granted, without the tooth problem.

Willow, in a slightly kinder tone, said, "I'm sure you were very thorough."

"Damn straight," Spike said. "Found another victim from those winged rats."

"Who?" Dawn said, looking disappointed. "Are you sure?"

Spike gave her a meaningful look. "Scads of twin puncture marks. Temples, neck, wrists. Dead only a couple of hours by the look of 'im. Few pints low in the blood department."

"Sounds like our minivamps," Buffy said, taking a toothpick from the box on the table and gingerly poking at a piece of chicken stuck between two teeth.

"Who was it this time?" Xander grimaced and crossed his arms over his chest. "Another hapless teenager filled with raging hormones?"

"Naw. Homeless man, I'd say. Probably a war vet. Found him in a tunnel about a block from Weatherly Park."

"Any sign of the teensies?" Buffy asked.

Spike pursed his lips. "Right after I found the bloke, I saw one of them little twinklies. Tried to follow it, but it disappeared through a grate in the sewer wall."

"I see. Also near the park, I suppose?" Giles asked. Spike nodded.

"Very well, then. It seems our work is cut out for us."

"So—what? We kill vampires?" Dawn asked. She glanced apologetically at Spike. "Little ones, I mean."

"But what should we use for weapons?" Willow said. "I'm not sure Mister Pointy will be of any use." She held up one of her chopsticks. "Even if we sharpened these, they'd be too big."

"Well, there's always holy water for starters," Tara offered.

"On it," Buffy said, holding out a large sports bottle filled with clear liquid. "Courtesy of Father Murphy."

"We have crosses," Anya said.

"But I'm thinkin' we can pretty much rule out crossbows," Xander said.

Giles frowned. "Which brings us back to stakes. We'll need something small enough to be effective on such a diminutive threat."

Buffy glanced from the bottle of holy water in one hand to the toothpick she still held in the other. She stabbed the toothpick into a half-eaten egg roll on a plate at the center of the table. "We'll improvise."

Spike rested his chin on his hand on the seat back. "We don't know where they are. Last time they came to us."

"Then we make them come to us again," Willow said.

Xander looked at her. "You're suggesting . . . ?"

"Bait," Willow said.

"Fine." Anya tried to sound confident. "I volunteer."

"No offense, Anya, but you don't exactly look like Helpless-Victim Girl," Buffy said. "And if these are the same fairies you knew, they may smell a trap."

"I'll do it," Willow offered.

Tara looked worried. "Willow, no!"

"Sounds like a plan," Buffy said.

Dawn leaned over to Spike and said, "At least you're safe from them. Tonight I'm going to wear long sleeves."

Buffy looked at her sister, knowing how close she had come to real danger the night before. Their mother would never have let Dawn go out with the Scoobies to set a trap at night, but Buffy felt no safer leaving her sister at home. As long as Dawn was with her, she could protect her sister. "Right," she said. "Everybody wears long sleeves and pants. No dresses."

"Guess my Dolce and Gabbana is out then," Xander quipped.

Willow grinned. "What about me? Shouldn't I be, you know, more baity?" She and Tara had each brought a change of sweaters and jeans to the debriefing, in case they were called upon to patrol.

"No problemo. Here's the plan," Buffy said, switching to commando mode. She asked Giles to drive her, Willow, Tara, and Dawn to her house, with a swing by Giles's apartment to pick up some clothes in basic burglar black. After everyone changed, Xander, Anya, and Spike would meet them at the park. "That's it, then," Buffy concluded. "See you all in thirty."

Half an hour later the Scoobies descended on Weatherly Park, which they had decided was the best venue for luring the fairies out. Buffy just hoped they wouldn't run into any garden-variety demons or vampires who might interfere with the plan.

Giles drove Willow, Tara, Dawn, and Buffy to Weatherly in his convertible. Unfortunately, there were several no-parking areas close to their chosen rendezvous, and Giles, not willing to risk another parking citation, was forced to drop his charges off and park more than a block away. He joined them a minute later.

All of them wore long sleeves and slacks and high-necked sweaters. The girls had their hair pulled into tight pony tails or braids.

All but Willow.

Everyone except Willow hid in bushes or behind trees. Meanwhile, the appointed Bait Girl, dressed in a skimpy sheath and strappy sandals from Buffy's closet, shivered slightly as she walked in circles in a grassy area of the park not far from where the dead couple had been found.

"Such a beautiful evening," Willow said to no one in particular. "Full moon. But I'm so . . . so lonely . . . walking all, um, *alone* here in the park." She whistled a rough approximation of "Blue Moon."

Beside Buffy, Dawn drew in a sharp breath. Buffy, squinting into the darkness, saw the flash of light just a few yards away from Willow. Then another flash, and another. Soon Willow's face was clearly visible in the magical glow of dozens of twinkling lights in gold, sil-ver, cherry, apricot, rose, brass, aqua, and purplish black. Willow seemed absolutely enchanted, as if she hadn't seen these fairies turn into vampires just the night before. Buffy hoped her friend was acting.

About twenty fairies gathered close to Willow, who seemed to be talking to them in a low, cooing voice.

Willow held up a cupped hand and several fairies landed in it, then took off again. A couple more fairies took their place. They too pushed off, executing aerial twirls in front of Willow's face. Soon there was a line of hovering, glowing fairies near Willow's hand. Each one in turn landed and took off again, performing some sort of airborne acrobatics solely for Willow's benefit. Willow smiled and swayed, as if to the rhythm of some unheard music. The fairies swirled about her in clouds now, and her eyes began to drift shut. Willow spoke to the creatures again, this time in a sharper tone.

"Wait for it," Buffy warned as Tara made an impatient move.

"That's it," Spike whispered. The change had been almost imperceptible. Buffy couldn't see the faces of the glowing tinks, but she saw the gem-toned translucent wings change to a spider web of black veins.

The microvamps swarmed around Willow. Hungry.

"Now," Buffy said.

Chapter Sixteen

Willow Rosenberg watched the charming, delicate fairies drifting around her like rainbow bits of dandelion fluff.

Communication here, Willow, she told herself. *Keep trying. Communication would be good.*

The melodic hum of beating wings changed to a menacing drone, like the buzz of twenty overgrown hornets. Instead of feeling afraid, a dreamy sort of lethargy settled over Willow. The fairies' eyes changed from lambent colors that matched their sheer clothing to pure black, and the ethereal creatures turned into vile, menacing bundles of evil on wings.

"I want to help you. I'm sure you all mean well. But, you know, not helping with the buzzing and the wrinkly forehead thing." She tried to back a step away but found that she was surrounded now by the fairy vamps. The buzzing grew louder. She held her hands up in front of her as if trying to hold them back, and spoke slowly, with great effort. "All right. It's only fair to warn you that I'm a powerful witch."

The buzzing drone quickly crescendoed to a whining, furious pitch. "Uh-oh. My bad," she said, her eyes flying open wide. Then, forcing herself back to full alertness, she realized something. "Hey . . . you—you understood me."

One of the vamps dove for her face. She swatted it away and sent it spinning through the air. "Back off. I was trying to give you a chance." More of the fluttering menaces appeared unexpectedly in the air beside her. "You think you're tough because you brought all your friends?" she asked. "Well, so did I."

The flitter critters did not back off. Instead, they swarmed around her, diving toward her exposed skin. And there was a lot of it. Willow heard a yell from the trees and bushes and knew her friends were on their way to help her. She shook her arms, dislodging several of the fairies, then grabbed one that had tangled itself in her hair and dashed it to the ground. Suddenly, Tara was there fighting alongside her, pulling the fanged marauders from her friend's hair and neck.

Some of the creatures were difficult to dislodge and left a bleeding needle-sharp trail of red on Willow's skin. "You're hurt," Tara said. She pulled out a toothpick and tried to jab at one of the little monsters, but it dodged out of the way.

Willow smacked one that was clinging to her cheek. "Just a scratch." It fell to the ground and lay there stunned. Tara stomped on it for good measure. "Tell me it's dead," Willow said. "Is it dead?"

Tara had no chance to answer as they were dive-bombed by a flock of the incoming teensies.

Spike raced beside the Slayer into the thick of battle.

"Dawn, stay with Spike," Buffy snapped. Then her eyes flashed toward Spike. "Keep her safe. Not a scratch on her."

The vampire quickly readjusted his priorities from impressing the Slayer to protecting Dawn, the most vulnerable of the Scooby gang. He couldn't keep her entirely from the battle. "Who do you think I am, Mary bloody Poppins?" he objected, but only for show. He knew he would protect Dawn no matter what it cost him. So did Buffy. "Come on," he said, grabbing Dawn's arm and pulling her to the edge of the fray.

Dawn yanked her arm away from him. "I don't need a baby-sitter."

"Course not, Nibblet," he agreed. "We're partners. You get my back, I get yours." He pulled a cigarette and lighter from his pocket, lit the cigarette, and handed the lighter to her. "Take this. Anyone comes near you, you fry 'em with that." He adjusted the lighter's flame control to high and held up a warning finger. "But I'll be behind you, so mind the hair and the jacket." He took a puff of the cigarette. Leaving it in his mouth, he got out two toothpicks, one for each hand. "Start at the outside. Pick off any stragglers, then we work our way toward center."

Dawn giggled. Spike glanced down at the toothpicks he held at the ready and realized how ridiculous he must look. "Bloody flying vermin," he said. "Can't even fight 'em without looking like some sort of poofter."

One of the glowing creatures flickered in front of him, and Spike lashed out with lightning fast reflexes and accuracy heightened by his anger. The light winked out and a puff of ash showered down on Spike and Dawn.

"Eew," said Dawn. "Come on, let's do it again."

A cluster of fairy vamps headed straight for Xander and Anya to head them off before they reached Willow. Xander lashed out at them with his toothpick-armed hands. They nimbly flew out of reach, then circled back to attack from behind. Anya punched one of them before it could bite the back of Xander's neck, where it was aiming for the hairline. "Go away!" Anya yelled. "If you hurt my boyfriend, I will hunt down every one of you flying shrimps."

Xander tried again with the toothpicks, but with no better result than the first time. The winged creatures were simply too fast. "All right then," he said, his face taking on a dangerous look. "Time to meet the Sunnydale welcoming committee." He flat-handed two of them, then pulled out the bottle of holy water that Buffy had given him.

Anya clapped her hands together, narrowly missed one fairy, then another. With the third smack of her palms she caught a minivamp. Its wings stopped fluttering instantly and it tumbled to the ground to lie motionless. "Welcome to Sunnydale. Now please leave," she said.

Xander unstoppered the sports bottle. A quartet of fanged creatures zoomed toward him and he squirted a stream of liquid into the air.

"No!" Anya said.

Xander's hand jerked and the stream went wide. "No? No what? Are you all right?" He looked at Anya, who stood mesmerized staring at a fairy vamp who shed a bright golden glow just inches from Anya's forehead.

"It's you. I remember," she said. Xander put a hand on Anya's arm as she spoke. "Mabyana. The queen of the fairy troop."

She seemed unable to move, and Xander felt a jab of alarm. "Ahn, snap out of it. Don't stare at them."

The fairy's wings made a sound like a diamond-back rattling. Xander pulled Anya back and aimed a squirt of holy water at the flying creature. With a flutter of its wings, it moved out of reach and seemed to buzz some sort of alarm. A dozen fairy vamps appeared as if from nowhere. Anya, no longer in a daze, swept her arms wide and brought them together again with a mighty smack of her hands. One fairy fluttered away with a broken wing. Xander opened fire with the holy water.

Most of the fairies flew clear of the water hazard, but the stream caught one of them full in the chest. For a moment it hung there with a sickening sizzle, and then burst into a ball of ash. "Kind of . . . gives a whole new meaning to the term fairy dust," Xander observed. He held the bottle high in front of them. "All right, who's next? Ring-around-the-rosy time."

One of the fairies Anya had stunned earlier shook itself and stood up on the ground. She stomped on it and it collapsed again. Suddenly, ten fairies had hold of Anya. One of them grabbed her ponytail. Five others attached themselves to various parts of her jacket and four grasped her pants legs. With a mighty heave, they lurched upward and Anya felt her feet leave the ground. "Xander!" she yelled, kicking her legs and jerking her arms, trying to pull free.

The fairies did not let go, but they could not seem to pull her more than a few inches off the ground. Another handful of fairy vamps approached from all directions.

"Hands off my girlfriend, microfreaks." Xander, knowing they could not hold his weight as well, threw himself at Anya in a flying tackle.

They fell to the ground, bursting the bottle of holy water beneath them as they fell. Tiny glowing vamps scattered in all directions.

A hissing, sizzling sound from beneath Anya told them that the spilled holy water had dispatched at least two more of the winged monsters.

Xander sucked in deep breaths of air. "Holy holy water, Batman. That was a close one."

Flipping end over end, Buffy made every part of her body a weapon. Her feet kicked small glowing balls high into the air. "Have patience with me."

Buffy's voice dripped mock sincerity. "I'm new to little guys." Her hands alternately slapped, flicked, smashed, or punched. "So I'm just *wing*ing it."

Giles stood nearby with a cross in one hand and a toothpick stake in the other. "Excellent agility training, I must say. You're really becoming quite accurate."

Buffy tucked and rolled beneath a trio of incoming fairies, then kicked up out of the roll, sending her enemies flying. Another one came at her and she whacked it hard with an elbow. It froze stunned in the air, and she smacked it to the ground with the flat of her palm. "If I'm so good," she panted, "how come there aren't any fewer of them than when we started?"

Giles blinked in surprise, then glanced around them. "Few—? I daresay there are more now than when we began."

Buffy drove back two more enemies with a pair of well-aimed punches. "I hope you don't mean they're multiplying," she said.

"Indeed not," Giles said, bringing his foot down on one of the fairies that had landed on the ground in front of him. "Merely that there may be more than we had originally anticipated." Holding the cross at head level, he knelt and examined the fairy he had stepped on. When it didn't move, he jabbed it with the toothpick for good measure and it poofed into a pile of dust.

Several fairies dove in toward Buffy in a V formation. She let loose with a flurry of kicks and punches. One of the fairies got past her guard and landed on Buffy's face. She hit the undeadette hard enough to stun it, and whacked her cheek in the process. Pain detonated in her jaw like a dental landmine going off. The vamp fell to the ground, but another dive-bombed the Slayer at eye level. Instinctively Buffy jerked away, still reeling from the pain, and lost her balance. A tree root caught her foot. She went down. Fresh agony drilled from her tooth straight up through her brain.

Giles fought his way over to Buffy and helped her up just as half a dozen fairies converged on their location. Shaking off the pain, Buffy stunned two, and the rest flew away to a distance to regroup. "Hate to be *picky,* but you're out of here." Overtaken with a need to be thorough, Buffy dusted the duo of stunned vamps with a toothpick stake from her pocket.

Spike and Dawn battled a cluster of minis with flame and stakes. One of them landed on Spike's leather duster, and he slapped a hand over it, trapping the creature. He squeezed and felt the thing wriggle and bite. Thinking quickly, Spike pinned the fairy in place with his thumb, then opened his hand and jabbed a toothpick through the microvamp's stomach and his own hand, effectively immobilizing his opponent and drawing blood from his palm. The tiny vamp began to lick at Spike's wound. In disgust, Spike flicked it in the head a few times to knock it unconscious.

"Some help over here," Xander called.

"Oh, dear," Giles said, hearing Xander's yell. More fairyvamps zoomed toward them. "Perhaps we should rethink our strategies."

Buffy ran to help and arrived just as Xander and Anya dove away from some attacking fairies and tumbled to the ground. She pulled her friends back to their feet.

Several groups of microvamps veered away from their intended targets.

"But look," Willow said. "We've got them on the run."

"Do we leave it as a rout?" Xander asked. "Or do we pursue and exterminate?"

At least three dozen of the glowing tinks were fleeing toward the bushes. "No time like the present," Buffy said.

Giles closed ranks with Spike and Dawn while Buffy, Xander, Anya, Tara, and Willow followed the fairies into a thicket of bushes. Dawn made a move to go after them, but Giles put a hand on her arm.

"We'll fight another day, Little Bit," Spike said, holding up his fisted right hand. "We've got what we need here."

Excitement showed in Dawn's eyes. "Buffy's going to be so surprised." The bushes shuddered and sounds of a scuffle drifted back to them. "Uh, oh," Dawn said when moments later the five Scooby defenders ran back out of the bushes pursued by at least a hundred twinkling lights.

Giles drew in a sharp breath. "Perhaps we should—"

"Run," Spike said.

The Slayerettes reunited as they ran en masse through Weatherly Park. "Willow, how's that teleportation spell you were practicing?" Buffy said.

"Yeah," Xander said. "Now's the time, if any, Will."

Tara panted. "It's all right. I'll help."

Without pausing, Willow lifted a hand overhead and gasped out the words of an incantation as she ran.

Tara kept one hand on Willow's shoulder and spoke the spell along with her, adding strength to her friend's power. An invisible ripple seemed to bounce from Willow's upstretched hand, and the creatures retreated ten feet as if from an electrical shock. Then, with an ominous angry buzz, all of the lights swirled up from the field of battle and winked out.

The gang kept running headlong out of the park.

"Wait." Willow stumbled to a halt, pressing her hands to her head. "And . . . *ow*."

"What's wrong?" Tara asked, looking worried. Willow groaned.

"What'd you put in that spell, Will, essence of hangover?" Xander asked, putting a steadying hand on her shoulder.

The rest of the gang stopped as well and turned back to help. Tara threw an arm around Willow's waist. "It was a pretty strong spell. I think she just overdid it."

"Get her to the car," Giles said.

"Which is where, exactly?" Xander glanced up and down the street.

Giles tilted his head to the left. "About a block that way."

"Then we'd better move before those microcreeps come back with reinforcements," Xander said. "I mean, game over, man. They kicked our butts."

"You okay?" Buffy asked, looking at Willow.

Willow nodded. "I just need to rest. No big." Her knees collapsed under her and Tara lost her balance.

Buffy grabbed Willow's arm, pulled her up, and put the arm over her shoulder so that Tara supported Willow from one side and Buffy from the other.

"No big, huh?" she said wryly. "I'd have to disagree with you there. That was our problem tonight. I don't think any of us were thinking small enough."

Giles had left the top to his convertible down, and when they got there, the friends quickly loaded the drooping Willow into it. Giles sped off with most of the girls in the car, leaving Xander, Spike, and Anya— who insisted on staying with the Xander—to walk warily back to the Summers house.

Spike, his right hand still clenched into a fist, carefully, guarded his winged prisoner.

Chapter Seventeen

Dawn leaned down to the sofa and handed two aspirin and a glass of water to Tara, who was sitting with Willow's head in her lap. "Thank you," Tara said. She helped Willow sit up just enough to take the tablets with a sip of water and eased her back down again.

Willow put a hand to her forehead. "Good thing I didn't waste that mini-teleportation spell on a bunch of dumb ants."

Tara stroked her friend's hair, wisely saying nothing.

"But we're glad you used it when you did," Dawn said.

Spike wandered into the room, his right hand loosely cupped, and sat in the stuffed chair at the end of the sofa. "Seems to have taken a lot out of you, Red. Afraid if you'd tried that in the middle of the fight you might've ended up as midnight munchies for our fine feathered *fiends*."

"There weren't any feathers," Dawn said. "I thought the wings were more—"

Spike gave her a you've-got-to-be-kidding look.

She stopped and held up an index finger. "Okay. Literary license. I get that."

"Where is everyone else?" Tara asked.

Anya entered from the dining room. "Mr. Giles is in the kitchen, and Xander took a breadboard, some large deli toothpicks, glue, and a diminutive drill into the basement. He said something about building a better mousetrap." She lowered her voice confidentially and sat cross-legged on the floor. "I don't know why we're interested in mice, but he's very sexy when he's working on a project."

Spike snorted.

"Buffy is upstairs in the bathroom," Dawn said. "She's been in there ever since we got home, running water in the sink and making weird gargly sounds." Her brows drew together. "Is it just me, or does something seem seriously wrong with my sister? Did you see when Buffy hurt herself during the fight and hit the ground? I couldn't believe it. I mean, Giles had to go help her up. I really think she's off her game."

"Maybe she's just worried about the fairies," Tara said.

"It's not that," Spike offered. "Goldie's got a gimp tooth."

"Bad," Willow muttered, trying to sit up. "That's

bad. Isn't that bad? She needs to do something about it."

Tara put a soothing hand on her head. "Shhhh."

"Doesn't know what to do. Bad tooth, no insurance." Spike shook his head. "Just trying to tough it out."

"Then obviously she should *pay* the dentist," Anya said as if the answer were obvious. "Dentists accept cash payments, don't they?"

Dawn looked down at the floor. "We, uh, don't really have much in the way of money. Mom didn't have a dental plan. She had life insurance, but the company said it could be two more months before they send the check. I don't understand it all."

"But," Tara stammered, "Buffy can't just let her tooth rot. Can she?"

"Do you think it might just get better on its own?" Dawn asked.

"Not likely," Spike said. "I think Big Sis has already tried everything she knows how, and it's gone from bad to worse."

Dawn looked over at Willow and Tara. "Do you know a spell maybe? Anything that could help?"

Willow sat up. "I think I know something."

"Honey, no," Tara said, trying to get her friend to lie back down again.

Willow gave her a wan smile. "Don't worry, there's no magick involved. Strictly unmagickal. Help for the hurtiness in Buffy's tooth."

"She's bloody stubborn," Spike said.

Dawn looked at him, her eyes widening in alarm. "Blood? Spike, I forgot. Your hand."

Spike gave her a sheepish look. "I was kind of waiting to show the Slayer."

"Show me what?" Buffy asked, coming down the stairs.

Spike held his right hand at chest level in front of himself and opened it slowly with his palm face up. Buffy's eyes went wide. "Oh . . . my . . . God! Spike, are you crazy?"

Spike looked nonplussed. "I knocked him out. He kept biting, so I had to, didn't I?"

Xander came up from the basement. "Buffy, do you have any bigger drill bits?" He stopped and stared at the vamp's hand. "You've had that stuck to you ever since we left the park?" Xander shook his head. "Of all the times I wished I could see Spike get *spiked,* this is not how I imagined it."

Giles rushed in from the kitchen to see what the commotion was about, a glass of juice in one hand and a half-eaten piece of toast in the other. "Dear me," he exclaimed, "whatever possessed you to drive a stake through your hand?"

Spike rolled his eyes. "It's hardly a stake. It's only a toothpick, init? Thought we could question the pernicious pest when he woke up," he said, nodding toward the tiny winged creature lying on his palm.

"Now Spikey, don't be disappointed if we can't let you keep it," Xander said in a paternal tone. "You know we'll just end up being the ones to feed it and clean up after it."

Spike ignored the interruption. "Any rate, if he came to before we got back here, I wasn't sure I could hang on to 'im. Dusted vamps don't talk. This one's a prisoner of war, I figure."

Buffy crossed her arms. "Why didn't you just put him in your pocket?"

"He'd have sliced through with his teeth in no time if he came round."

"Yes, I suppose he's right," Giles said. "Thank you, Spike. That was very . . . practical of you. But it may be advisable to transfer our captive now. Dawn, do you have a glass jar perhaps . . . a piece of cardboard?"

"I have some foam board," Dawn said. "Left over from my science project."

"Yes, I'd say that should do." Giles took a bite of toast and chewed thoughtfully. "Unfortunately, I'm not at all sure we'll be able to communicate with our . . . winged houseguest once he wakes up."

"Of course we can," Anya said. "Fairies always speak some of the language of the country they're in."

Buffy raised a skeptical eyebrow at Anya. "And would that be Spanish or English, then?"

"Probably English," Anya said, "and of course Italian, since this troop came from Italy." She smiled proudly. "Giles and Spike and I all speak Italian, and I know a few words of fairy-speak." She spread her hands eagerly. "So now all we need is a conscious fairy."

Xander frowned. "How do we even know it's going to wake up?" he said. "What if it's dead already?"

"No poof," Willow said from the sofa. "Wouldn't there be a poof?"

Buffy gave an emphatic nod. "I killed some. There was definite poofage. So what's the deal with Sleeping Beauty, then?"

"Already on it," Spike said. He got up and went into the kitchen and returned to the living room coffee table with a towel, a bowl of water, a sponge, and some toothpicks. When Dawn brought in the square of foam board, he transferred the toothpick-pinned fairy from his hand to the slab of foam. Spreading out the towel on the table, he placed the foam square on top of it.

"On it? By doing what?" Buffy asked. "Giving the thing a bath?"

"This little 'n's slept long enough," Spike said. "Waiting's over." He dipped the sponge into water and held it above the immobilized fairy, letting a few drops splat onto the creature's upturned face. The wings trembled. The fairy spluttered, shook its head, and opened its eyes. The humans and vampire gathered into a tight semicircle and peered down at it.

The fairy, a tiny, perfect man-shaped sprite, had silver hair that stuck out in stylish spikes, making him look like a miniature rock star. Except, of course, for the translucent pairs of oval wings and the lavender tights and jerkin that brought out the enchanting lavender of his eyes.

"Weird." Dawn stared in fascination. "How do you interrogate a fairy?"

"We could try playing a few Celine Dion albums." Xander wore a mischievous smile. "How long could any prisoner hold out? If that doesn't work, we switch to Don Ho."

The fairy chittered frantically and threw its arms across its face. It tried to push itself up to fly and then for the first time seemed to notice the stake that held it pinned down to the foam slab. His hands reached for the toothpick and strained to pull it out, but to no avail.

"If Anya is right, then this fairy should be able to understand and respond to everything we say." Giles pressed a finger thoughtfully to his chin.

"Yup. In the park, I'm sure they understood me," Willow said.

Spike placed a black-fingernailed hand on either side of the prisoner. "All right, then, spill it. Tell us what you lot are up to, or I relocate that wooden stake to the center of your heart."

Giles adjusted his glasses, leaned forward, and spoke in a kindly tone. "Well, hello."

Spike cleared his throat. "Kind of gettin' in the way of my bad cop thing here, if you take my meaning."

"Oh, sorry." Giles straightened and Buffy leaned close to the fairy.

"Hi, I'm Buffy," she said. "And you're in big trouble."

"Tell us who you are," Xander added. "And that's just for starters. Don't try to pull any of that name, rank, and serial number crap. The Geneva Convention doesn't apply to fairies."

The lavender-clothed fairy shook its head, as if confused. "*Mi chiamo Lucket. Abbiamo bisogno d'un interprete.*"

"Actually, Lucket, we have three interpreters here.

But we don't *need* one." Anya's voice was matter-of-fact and dangerous. "Cut the theatrics and speak English. We know you can, so don't force us to use violence."

The creature made a buzzing, hissing sound, then said one distinct word. "Demon."

"Oh," she said with pleased surprise. "You remember me?"

The fairy's voice was high-pitched and slightly softer than a human's, as if the creature had just taken a breath from a helium balloon, but still distinct and audible. Stranger still, he sounded as if he had learned English from Italian immigrants in New Jersey— which perhaps he had. "Yeah, I remember you. Not one of our troop has ever forgotten you or that scum sorceress Devara. Hundreds of years ago you took the joy outta our lives, cursed us with the reality we gotta deal with now."

Anya spluttered. "Me? I never cursed you. I shattered a vampire demon. And anyway, I was only doing my job. There was certainly nothing personal about it. Devara was the one who sent the demon into the fairy troop."

"So whatever happened to the sorceress?" Dawn asked.

"Oh," Anya said, "she fell in love again, married, and had a child. Although I heard they all drowned in a well ten years later. Some sort of freak accident."

Buffy looked skeptically at Anya. "Or not."

The fairy buzzed with scorn. "It was the perfect trap. What woman wouldn't fall for it—her tortured husband

and son yellin' for help from the bottom of a well?"

"Not very sporting, was it, then?" asked Spike, then muttered, "Wish I'd thought of that."

Buffy scowled at him. "Why don't you two killers just spend a little time swapping tricks of the trade. Don't let those of us with beating, caring hearts stop you."

Spike looked taken aback. "I'm just saying, Love, there's a certain artistry . . ." His voice trailed off.

"Watch your back, Cookie," the fairy warned Anya. "The smart money says you're next." With that, he fell silent and refused to say another word.

Vesuva, her black-light glow completely damped, pressed against the window and watched the human monsters conduct their interrogation. Because she had seen the blond vampire capture Lucket, she followed the vamp as he left the battle, hoping to find a way to rescue her friend. No opportunity had presented itself. Lucket was trapped inside the house, Vesuva trapped outside.

So Vesuva had listened. Queen Mabyana would be most interested in what the human monsters said.

Someone in the house pulled the curtains shut. But the humans could not stay inside forever.

Vesuva would recommend that the queen post scouts near the house. That way, if any of the monsters ventured forth, the scouts could alert the rest of the troop and take the necessary action.

Vesuva raced off to inform the Fairy Queen.

Chapter Eighteen

Queen Mabyana was not amused when Vesuva reported that the oafish humans had actually captured one of her followers. She tossed her glowing golden hair and flounced the skirt of her sheer spring-leaf green dress. How *dare* they? Lucket was a favorite of hers. Mab's forehead went all vamp-wrinkly at the very thought. More than a dozen members of her troop had been reduced to piles of dust by a few witless humans and a traitorous vampire. That hurt. Why did no one ever stop to consider *her* feelings? Of course she could try to be brave, put a good face on things, but Mab's troop needed revenge. Again.

They started their mischief slowly while she gave herself time to form a plan. It was simple enough to let the air out of hundreds of car tires along the street.

Next they dispersed to fly above countless houses, sending nightmares to any animal or child sleeping inside them. Several of her lieutenants set off fire alarms at schools, city hall, hotels, and even the hospital.

The Fairy Queen herself found a can of gasoline outside a small shed in a backyard, touched a spark to it, and watched it explode into flames. The fire department, already busy with an overwhelming number of false alarms, would certainly arrive too late.

Steet, in a moment of inspiration, took several fairy vamps with him and hovered above a set of power lines. His cherry punk-cut hair shone brightly in the darkness. Under their combined mental efforts, the lines split and the ends swung sparking toward the ground. Block after block of houses was plunged into darkness.

Swarming toward downtown, the fairies wreaked more mischief. Dorse, a streak of glowing aqua, landed on a traffic signal, turning the red light to green in midcycle. Inattentive drivers powered into the intersection, only to be broadsided by cross traffic. Metal crunched and shrieked. Glass shattered. Horns blared.

Droplets of blood spattered one of the windshields, but Mab wasn't satisfied yet. She had almost convinced herself that there was no point in holding a grudge against a demon who probably didn't exist anymore—a demon who had turned her once merry and idyllic life with a flock of countless delightful adorers into an unending nightmare of bloodthirst.

But tonight the Fairy Queen had seen the demon

again. Not overly surprising, now that she thought about it, since this town was the center of some sort of mystical convergence. It had drawn Mabyana and her troop here. Why not a demon?

Now Mab's grudge was back full force. Her Fair Ones had almost managed to nab Anyanka, but that cloddish male had interfered. The "boyfriend." It was only a temporary setback, though. Mab, the golden queen, could be as versatile as she was beautiful. Punishment could come in many forms—and Anyanka certainly had it coming. Mab had never asked for any role other than that of beloved ruler of her Fair Folk. Still, as long as she had been turned into the Fairy Shrew of the Universe, she would do what came naturally. Mab refused to lose any more of her troop—to demons *or* to humans.

Mab had a plan now for settling an old, old score. The fact that Vesuva had given her the idea completely slipped her mind. The fairies would need to act soon, so she signaled for her troop to gather. They would like her plan. There was a certain simple charm to it.

Chapter Nineteen

The next couple of hours at the Summers house were spent in a variety of post-slayer activities. Lucket was placed in solitary confinement in the dining room. In spite of the very real possibility of another attack by the microvamps on an innocent victim, the Scoobies knew their first plan had failed, and they needed time for the three R's: research, rest, and reorganization. Not to mention better weapons and a new strategy.

Tara made several phone calls while Willow rested on the couch. Xander returned to his work in the basement. Giles checked Anya for injuries. Her wrist was swollen, probably injured as Xander tackled Anya to free her when the fairy vamps tried to carry her off. She had hardly noticed the pain in the mad rush from Weatherly Park to Buffy's house, but now it had begun to throb and ache. Giles applied an ice pack and wrapped the wrist with an elastic sports bandage.

"Thank you," Anya said. "I'm sure you would have made an excellent doctor. Doctors earn a great deal of money."

Giles gave her a self-deprecating smile. "Yes, well, rest assured it's all part of a watcher's duties. In my capacity as a field medic, I'm largely paid for by the benevolence of the Watcher's Council." He pushed his glasses up higher on his nose. "Even if I weren't, I should be very foolish indeed not to safeguard the health of my finest employee."

Anya beamed. "Thank you. And my pride in your compliment is in no way diminished by the fact that I'm your only employee." She frowned. "But my wrist still hurts. When will it stop hurting? I don't like injuries."

"Er, it may actually take some time," Giles began earnestly.

"Here, try this," Dawn said. She shook two more aspirin from the bottle on the coffee table and handed them to Anya. "Specialty of the day." She held the bottle up. "Anyone else?"

"Oh, me! Me!" Buffy said, walking into the room.

Giles looked at her in surprise. "Were you hurt during the fight?"

She made an airy gesture with one hand. "Of course not. You know me, I'm just a sucker for the house special. Water anyone?" she said, quickly changing the subject. "Comes with free ice cubes."

"I already have ice, thank you," Anya said, pointing to the cold pack on her wrist.

Tara nodded. "I think Willow could use some more."

Spike looked up from the chair beside the sofa. "Don't suppose you've got a nice single-malt Scotch laying about?"

Buffy gave him a withering look. Spike pressed his lips together and outward. "Right, then." He pulled a flask from his jacket pocket, unscrewed the cap, and took a gulp.

Giles got up from his kneeling position beside Anya. "I'll help you with the glasses, Buffy."

It was nearly midnight by the time Xander came back upstairs carrying the transformed paddle-shaped breadboard and eating a Hershey bar.

"What is that?" Buffy said, looking at his invention.

Ever helpful, Anya answered for him. "It's chocolate," she said. She looked at Xander. "Is it bait for the better mousetrap you built?"

Dawn raised a corner of her mouth. "Looks like a porcupine that got run over by a steam roller—backward."

"Could be a hairbrush for a Gnoxl demon," Buffy suggested.

Spike quirked a brown eyebrow. "Naw. Prob'ly just a back scratcher for Carpentry Boy."

Xander looked as if he were tempted to hit Spike with the augmented breadboard. "Well at least I was doing something more useful than getting drunk and waiting for some uncooperative insect to talk."

"I believe insects have six legs," Anya said.

Xander ignored the comment. "Other than taking a useless prisoner, what have you done to help?"

Spike gave Xander a challenging look. "Dusted five wingies myself tonight. How many did you kill?"

Xander's eyes slid away from Spike's. "Behold how impressed I'm *not*. You see, I'm not living in the past here. Sure, you had the edge at the park tonight, but all that is about to change. I'm looking toward the future."

"Just tell us what you made, Xander," Buffy said.

Xander hefted the paddle breadboard to show them the miniature defoliated forest of deli toothpicks sprouting from its flat surface. He had drilled wide vent holes between the potentially lethal rows of diminutive stakes. "Had to do a bit of Frankensteining, but what you see before you, my friends, is the all new and improved Slayomatic." He swung it as if it were a baseball bat aimed at an oncoming pitch. "Figured those little nasties were too fast for most of us to be really accurate tonight. But with this baby"—he swung again and stopped abruptly as if he had connected with an invisible baseball— "mere accuracy becomes irrelevant."

Giles's eyebrows rose in an intrigued expression. "Excellent. I daresay you might dispatch quite a few that way." He sighed. "And there do seem to *be* quite a few."

"Yeah, what was with that?" Buffy asked. "On Friday night there were maybe twenty; tonight a few more, maybe, but nothing knee-shivering. Then a few more and a few more and all of a sudden, *bam*. Ambush in the, uh, bushes."

"There were over a hundred," Willow said from the sofa. "I started to count, but I sort of lost track with the running and the teleportation and—"

"And the stumbling and the headaching," Tara added.

"Right," Giles said. "Well, we've no idea how many fairies are actually in this troop."

"The original troop in Italy had at least a thousand fairies," Anya said.

Giles removed his glasses.

"And we're sure these are the same vampettes?" Buffy asked.

"Lucket definitely knows who I am. And I recognized their queen in the park during the fight," Anya said. "She seemed very angry."

Xander sighed. "So they tried to whisk you off to Neverland for a little party, huh?"

"I don't know why," Anya said. "I've never done anything to hurt them."

Buffy looked at her in disbelief. "You mean *other* than trying to kill them tonight?"

"Plus, you know, the making it possible for them to become vampires in the first place?" Willow said.

Anya looked genuinely confused. "I was only doing my job. There was nothing personal."

"Looks like somebody took it personal," Spike said.

"So what are we saying?" Tara asked. "Anya has

all these enemies she didn't know about, and there could be a thousand of these things?"

The corner of Buffy's mouth twitched downward. "I know. Kind of makes you tired just thinking about it."

"Indeed," Giles said. "I believe we could all benefit from some rest. We'll formulate a new—and preferably more effective—plan in the morning."

Dawn and Buffy passed out pillows, blankets, and sleeping bags.

Tara's face was uneasy. "The fairies are still out there."

"And they haven't eaten," Willow added sleepily. "I hope no one else gets hurt."

"That's a lot of mouths to feed," Spike mused.

Chapter Twenty

Xander woke up at five A.M. with a kink in his neck from lying on the sofa with Anya. He disentangled himself from his sleeping girlfriend, careful not to jostle her bandaged wrist, stood, and rubbed his neck. Giles was in a sleeping bag on the floor on the other side of the coffee table, and Spike was dozing in his chair. There was no sign of Buffy, Dawn, Tara, or Willow, so Xander assumed they all must have gone upstairs to sleep. It was still dark outside.

Knowing he would never get back to sleep himself, Xander headed upstairs for a quick shower and dressed again in the clothes he had worn all night. Then he went into the kitchen to check out what breakfast supplies the Summers household held. The results of his search were not terribly encouraging. In the refrigerator he found a pair of eggs, a trickle of orange juice at the bottom of an orange plastic bottle, a cup or so of milk already a day past its sell-by date, and half a stick of butter. The pantry did not yield much more. The four cereal boxes there were almost entirely empty.

He shook his head. "Ah, Captain Crunch, I hardly knew ye." There was no bread at all, and he found the empty bread wrapper in the trash. So, no hope of French toast either. He set his jaw decisively and murmured, "No one's gonna starve on my watch." He would have to go foraging for food. Maybe there would be time to swing by home for a change of clothes, as well. He scribbled a quick message to Anya—*Getting breakfast, etc. Back by seven. XOXOX, Xander*—and set up a pot of coffee that he would begin brewing as soon as he returned.

The clocks had recently been set for daylight-saving time, and it was still quite dark outside. Xander wasn't sure exactly when the sun would rise, but it could be as much as an hour away. The microvamps would be nuts to be out so close to daybreak, but he decided to take along a cross and a few toothpicks as a precaution.

With that, he pulled on a jacket and slipped out of the house into the cool predawn air. Holding the cross in one hand, he stayed alert for any danger. The streets of Sunnydale were quiet, and Xander enjoyed the solitude as he walked briskly to the donut shop. Once there, he slid the cross into his back pocket. He enjoyed picking out treats for his friends. Chocolate cake with sprinkles for Dawn, a bear claw for Anya, a cruller for Willow. Oddly, he couldn't remember what kind of donuts Tara liked, so he threw in several extra raised glazed and a couple of custard-filled. They seemed like her.

Of course there were raspberry jelly-filled for Buffy and Giles—and, he supposed, for Spike. For good measure, he added a couple of cinnamon rolls, a maple bar, some powdered sugar donuts, three glazed old-fashioned buttermilk, and two dozen assorted donut holes for variety. Enough carbs to fuel even the most strenuous of vampire hunts.

He paid and left the donut shop with a largish pink box that held his breakfast treasures. The sun would rise soon and any Sunday-morning commuters would throw themselves into the congestion of Southern California traffic, but for now all was peaceful. Xander's stomach growled. Deciding against going back to the apartment to change clothes, he crossed the street and headed back toward Buffy's house. As always, there was a headiness to holding all that gooey sweetness right in his hands.

As he walked, he eased one flap of the box open, slid his hand inside, and pulled out a donut hole. He had just popped the powdered sugar morsel into his mouth and begun to chew when a faint glimmer caught his eye behind a hedge off to his right. He turned his head to look directly at it, but saw nothing. A light flickered at the left corner of his vision. His head snapped back toward it. Again nothing.

"Gas light treatment, huh? I getcha," Xander said, starting to feel uneasy. Sunrise could not be more than fifteen minutes away. The fairies would never risk being out at this hour. Would they?

Another glint, at the upper edge of his peripheral vision this time. Xander finished chewing and swallowed hard. As much as he hated to admit it, it might not have been a bad idea to have wakened Spike and brought him along. In a perverse way, the undead did occasionally make good companions. Microvamps might just be less likely to attack the Big Bad.

A low humming thrummed in the air, not quite ominous. A small fairy sprang into view in full cherry-red glow just out of arm's reach in front of Xander. A second, third, and fourth joined it, flying in a loose semicircle just above the donut box. Magenta, indigo, cherry, and apricot light glimmered in the darkness.

Xander froze. "Now look, I'm sure last night was all a big misunderstanding." He edged sideways and tried to go around the fairies, but they moved with him. Xander watched in uncomfortable amazement as one of the winged imps landed on the far corner of the donut box and executed a series of handsprings, cartwheels, and somersaults diagonally across the box. "And the Russian judge gives it a five point two," he muttered.

A second glowing sprite landed on the opposite far corner and performed its own tumbling run across the box. Now there were two fairies at each of the corners closest to Xander. "Now, guys," Xander said, grinning nervously, "it's not that I don't appreciate the artistic quality of what you're doing here—because I do—but I really need to be getting back now."

Suddenly a fairy was at each of the four corners of the donut box trying to lift it from his arms. Xander tightened his grasp and yanked it back. "Oh, no, you'll have to do a little bit more than dance for your breakfast. If you guys are hungry, you'll have to—" He stopped short. If these microvamps were hungry, they would not be satisfied with donuts.

He quickly changed his tune. "Or maybe we could work out a compromise." He pulled out a chocolate donut hole and thrust it at the nearest fairy. The apricot-haired tink grabbed it, although it was almost as large as she was, holding it easily as if it were a gigantic beach ball. The fairy tasted it, chittered something to her companions, and threw the donut hole to the ground.

Now a dozen more fairies winked into view, moving to form a circle around Xander. Several of them held tangles of something Xander could not identify. All at once, the fairies surrounding him transformed into miniature flying vampires with bumpy foreheads, sharp teeth, and black-veined wings.

"Not good," Xander muttered. "This can never be good." He took an uncertain step backward and bumped into two fairies who immediately began yanking at his short dark hair. He held the box with one hand and batted at the fairies with the other, trying to loosen their hold. He realized that he had made another fatal error, one that a soldier should never make: He had entered a combat zone woefully unprepared. His meager weapons seemed little better than nothing at all.

Holding the donut box with one hand, Xander took out a toothpick and jabbed it toward the nearest flitter-vamp. He missed. Oddly, the creatures seemed bolder, less fearful than the evening before. Two of them flew at the toothpick from either side, grabbed it, and yanked it from his fingers. He reached for the other toothpick, fumbled, and heard it fall with a click onto the sidewalk. Not good. A fairy whisked the weapon away before he could recover it.

Xander pulled the cross from his back pocket. He swung at a group of fairies, but only managed to hit one. Something pushed him from behind. He tried to keep his balance while juggling the cross and the donut box, but the cross flew from his hand and landed under a bush.

In desperation, he ripped open the pink box and lobbed a raised glazed donut at a fairy at one o'clock. The fairy flew backward, clutching the hurled wheel of pastry for dear life. Xander grabbed the bear claw, put it back, and tossed a cruller instead.

"Abandoning plan A entirely, he moves into plan B," Xander said aloud. This was followed by a maple bar and then a powdered-sugar. He nodded as it hit and another fairy went spinning out of control, completely covered in white. "Another one bites the dust."

More fairies appeared, tugging at his sleeves, yanking at his hair. Xander picked up a jelly-filled donut and smashed it over the head of one that was standing on his arm. Completely engulfed by the cake and its sweet red gooeyness, the fairy plummeted to the ground. The melodic hum changed to a menacing buzzing sound, and fairy lights winked on and off all around him as if they were trying to confuse and distract him.

Xander blinked, trying to focus on his individual enemies. *Sunrise must be no more than ten minutes from now.* If he could just hold out, the fairies would be forced to flee just to escape the sunlight. Xander concentrated. He hurled another donut, then another donut, then another, hitting as often as he missed. He wished fervently that he had thought to bring the Slayomatic along with him as a precaution. He felt a sting on his ear and knew that he had been bitten. Fortunately, none of the fairies had yet gone for the exposed portion of his neck above his dark sweater at the opening of his jacket.

He was almost out of donuts and switched to donut holes, though these were less accurate and had much less of an impact. Smashing them into the faces of the vamps on his arms and head seemed to be the most effective use. While he practiced precision mashing, a handful of fairy vamps formed a line at the periphery of the battle as if just waiting for him to run out of ammunition. This happened far too quickly. At last he was left with only the bear claw. He felt dizzy from the exertion. He wasn't sure how, but now there were blinking, winking lights everywhere around him, dozens and dozens.

"Sorry, Ahn," he said, and he took a quick bite of the bear claw and flung it defiantly at a cluster of fairies. He was about to drop the empty box, but on inspiration scooped it through the air like a steam

shovel and slapped down the top, trapping a cluster of
glowing monsters. He dropped the box to the ground
and stamped on it hard. Then, like a beleaguered quar-
terback running for the end zone, he tried to break
through the cordon of fairies—only to be yanked back
by countless tiny hands on his jacket, pants, and hair.

There were enough of the fairies to hold him
immobile now, and the ones that had been hovering at
the edge of the battle swept in, holding something
between them. Several pairs split off. One of the pairs
flew behind Xander, the other in front of him. They
crisscrossed and flew in opposite circles around him.
Xander felt something yank tight around his arms and
looked down to see that it was a string of some sort.
They were tying him up!

His arms were pinned to his sides above the
elbows, and he tried to bring his hands up to pull the
string away, but the fairies' grasp on him was too tight.
The second pair of fairies wrapped their makeshift
string around his forearms and a third set around his
ankles. The string seemed to be made up of a hodge-
podge of twine, kite strings, shoestrings, yarn, rope,
and fishing line, all tied together. From the smell of it,
the bits and pieces had recently been salvaged from a
garbage heap or the sewer.

Panic rose inside Xander. "Ever considered picking on someone your own size?" The fairies flew in
faster and faster circles around him with their string,
tying him up ever more tightly. "Oh, no. Not liking the
whole Gulliver thing here," Xander said.

When the string fairies had used up their line, they

flew in intricate patterns around each other, tying the ends into knots. While they were putting on the final touches, several other fairies, buzzing with anger, flew up to Xander's eye level and pelted him with pieces of donut. One of them smashed a donut hole into his ear. Another stuffed a piece of raised glazed up his left nostril.

A pair of fairies, one of them covered in red slime, approached him with a mashed jelly donut and flew straight toward his mouth. Something moved on its surface, and Xander shuddered. "Oh, no. Not with the ants, now. No ants." He pressed his lips shut and furiously blew air out through his nose. The piece of raised glazed shot from his left nostril and struck one of the jelly donut–toting fairies. Two more glowing vamps joined the effort, but Xander refused to open his mouth and the angry fairies had to content themselves with mashing the mangled donut against his lips and chin.

Xander shook his head to dislodge it. He could feel the sticky smears of red on his mouth. An ant crawled across his upper lip and several more up his cheek. He tried again to pull his legs apart or raise his arms, hoping to break the makeshift bonds that held him, but the fairy string held tight.

A swarm of fairies flew at him from the front and pushed. Xander fell over like a long bowling pin struck by a twenty-pound ball. His head struck the sidewalk, and the world turned a fuzzy gray. Through blurred vision, he saw the swarms of tiny lights spread out all across his body, taking hold of clothing or string. Several tiny hands grasped his hair, and then he felt himself lifted free of the sidewalk.

"Great. You couldn't have just picked me up without knocking me down first?" he grumbled. Then the world dissolved into blackness.

Chapter Twenty-One

The living room of the Summers house was filled to capacity with bleary-eyed Scoobies when the telephone rang. Buffy, lying on the carpet, head on her arms, said, "Only a sadist would call at eight A.M. on a Sunday."

"I'll get it," Anya said, running to answer the phone. "Probably Xander. He must have been gone for hours by now." She grabbed it with her uninjured hand. "The sofa was very lonely without you," she said into the receiver. She paused. "Oh. I see. I was expecting my boyfriend Xander. Oh? Well, she doesn't actually live here, but I can get her for you." She held up the phone. "Willow, a strange woman is asking to speak with you."

Willow and Tara exchanged a knowing look.

Buffy forced herself into a sitting position and watched the red-haired wiccan cross to the telephone. "Who would be calling Willow here? Especially at this hour." It couldn't be Willow's mother, or Anya wouldn't have referred to the caller as a stranger. But why would a stranger call Willow at Buffy's house?

"It's me," Willow said into the phone. She listened for a minute. "Today? No, that's great. Perfect. We'll . . . we'll take it. Half an hour? She'll be there. Thank you." Willow hung up the phone. She turned to the room with a triumphant smile on her face. "That was Doctor Wilson."

"Doctor?" Buffy said. "Is somebody sick?"

Dawn, sitting on the floor with her back against the sofa, looked at her sister. "We know, Buffy."

"Know what?"

"About your tooth."

Buffy's eyes narrowed, and she slid a poisonous glance at Spike. "You sniveling, traitorous, sneaking son of a—"

"Hold on now. I never snivel," Spike said defensively.

"No, no, no," Willow said. "Not with the finger pointing."

Tara gave Buffy a placating smile. "Dawn was really worried. Spike was only trying to help."

Buffy scowled. "Worried? What was there to worry about? It's just a little toothache."

"Come on, Buffy," Willow said. "We've all noticed you've kind of been not so much with the perkiness of slayering. Well, you know what I mean."

Dawn sighed. "You made mistakes. And you weren't eating. And you kept going off by yourself."

Buffy tried to think of an argument against this,

but Spike rolled his eyes. "Face it, Blondie, you're hardly firing on all thrusters."

Willow made a frustrated sound. "We don't have time to argue. Doctor Wilson has agreed to see Buffy in half an hour at the student health center at UC Sunnydale."

Buffy blanched. "Uh, Willow, that's really nice of you, but I can't, I mean I'm not a student there any—I mean . . ." Her voice trailed off.

Willow gestured with her hands. "It's okay, Buffy. She's going to treat you for free as a favor to me, to us. Well, maybe more as a favor in return for a favor. You see, Doctor Wilson's a single mother." Buffy frowned in confusion at this nonsequitur.

"Her son David is in a class with Willow and me. He wants to be a veterinarian," Tara said helpfully. "So last night I called David and explained the situation."

"You know, with your mother dying and with the trying to make ends meet and with the trying to run a household," Willow said. "Anyway, when we called again, David said his mom had agreed to treat you for free if one of us would help him study today for his veterinary entrance exam."

Tara shrugged. "I volunteered. After that, all we needed was a time for Doctor Wilson to see you. She's making time in half an hour."

Buffy smiled at her friends but was still reluctant. "That's really great of you guys, but I can't see a dentist now. We have priorities. There are killer pixies on the loose. We have to figure out where they're hiding and how to get rid of them, and Xander might be missing."

Anya looked really alarmed now.

Dawn looked suspicious. "Buffy, are you *afraid* to go to the dentist? I mean, sure you fight vampires and werewolves and evil and all its forms . . ."

"Dentists are not evil," Anya said. Then her expression changed to panic. "Do you really think something happened to Xander? He's been gone way too long."

"We'll find him," Willow assured her.

"You know, dentists do have those pointy drills and all," Dawn said, changing the subject back to Buffy. "Could be pretty scary."

"I'm not afraid of the dentist," Buffy said. "But I can't just think of myself at a time like this."

"Buffy," Giles broke in, "you're most valuable to us when you're in top fighting form. Others can look for Xander and continue the research without you. But when it comes time for the final fight, we'll need you at your best."

"Any rate, Love, has your tooth gotten any better?" Spike asked.

"No," Buffy admitted, "it's worse."

"Come on," Dawn said, her eyes pleading with Buffy. "It's free. Free is good."

"Free is good," Buffy agreed.

"I can drive you and Tara to the university in my car," Giles offered. "I wanted to stop by the Magic Box anyway to pick up a couple of books. I can read them while I'm waiting."

"See?" Willow said. "Anya and I will find Xander, and then make with the research while you're gone."

"I'm planning another heart-to-heart with our prisoner in there," Spike said, indicating the fairy in the dining room.

Dawn's voice was wheedling. "And I'll study history."

Seeing herself completely outnumbered, Buffy gave in.

Lying back in the dental chair, Buffy's mouth was open wider than she ever remembered having to open it, as wide as the mouth of the Tyrloch demon she'd spiked down the throat. She looked up into Dr. Wilson's intent dark face. "Is iss oing to take ong?" Buffy asked, speaking around the pick and mirror the dentist was using to examine her tooth.

"Patience, child," Dr. Wilson said. "I've got to see what's goin' on here first." She poked and prodded, and Buffy had to force herself not to squirm. Dr. Wilson made a clucking sound and shook her head, making her cornrowed braids swing back and forth. "You're lucky you didn't let this go on any longer or we might be doing a root canal here. Sometimes that's the only way to get rid of the problem. My mom always told me, 'You take good care of your teeth, they take good care of you.' Looks to me like you didn't listen what your teeth were tryin' to tell you."

"An you fiss it?"

"'Course I can fix it," the dentist said with a laugh. "Take me an hour, maybe hour and a half."

Buffy tried to sit up and protest. Dr. Wilson pushed her back down. "We don't take care of this now, you'll be back for three, maybe four hours of work—and *that* won't be free. You take your choice."

Buffy forced herself to relax back into the chair. Though still mumbling through Dr. Wilson's fingers, she tried to sound upbeat and cheerful. "Dus diss invov dwills an udder pointy odjex?"

Dr. Wilson raised one dark eyebrow. "You're in a dentist's office. When does that not involve pointy things?" She picked up a syringe with an extremely long needle on it. "You'll feel a little pinch at first, but soon you're gonna feel a whole lot better."

Chapter Twenty-Two

By eight-thirty A.M. it was painfully clear that something had gone wrong for Xander. Far more painful than Anya's injured wrist. Anya phoned their apartment first, but only the answering machine picked up. Next she opened the yellow pages and found the phone number for the donut shop Xander frequented. The counter girl who answered the telephone had only come on duty at eight A.M. The baker had been in the kitchen since three and had seen nothing. Anya pressed the girl anyway, describing Xander in excruciating detail until she finally offered to have the clerk from the graveyard shift call Anya.

Ten minutes later the phone rang and it was the night clerk. Anya again described her boyfriend and asked if the man had seen him. "Look, lady," the clerk replied with a sigh, "Sunday morning's a busy time, what with the churches getting donuts and refreshments for their fellowship hours and what have you. I musta had sixty customers between five and eight o'clock this morning. And that's not even counting the cops who stop in for coffee and a chat over donuts. I seen plenty of young white guys today come into the shop, and yeah, one of 'em *might* have been your boyfriend, but that's all I can say."

Anya hung up, so distracted by worry that she forgot to thank the man or insincerely wish him a nice day. She sat down on the living-room couch surrounded by the remaining Scoobies, leaned forward with a sigh, and put her head in her hands. This made her bandaged wrist ache, and she was once again reminded of the frailty of these mortal bodies they all wore. "If anything's happened to Xander—"

"If?" Spike's voice was heavy with sarcasm. "We're long beyond *if,* aren't we, pet? Might as well admit that Lover Boy's gone missing. Maybe he found some other beautiful ex-demon and ran off with her." He was in a dark mood after his most recent attempt at fairy interrogation had yielded nothing.

Willow, ever the comforter, moved over beside Anya and put an arm around her. "Don't worry. We haven't lost Xander yet." Anya turned her head slightly to look at the red-haired girl. "Well," Willow fumbled, "not permanently, anyway. And Xander's pretty good at taking care of himself. He's clocked years of field time with the Slayerettes."

"You're trying to comfort me," said Anya. "But you've got worry face. Your eyebrows, your forehead. You can't hide worry face from me."

"Maybe we should look for him," Willow said. "We could start at the donut shop if you like. I'll go with you, Anya."

"Me too," Dawn said.

"No," Spike, Anya, and Willow said in unison.

"You promised to study history," Willow said.

"Buffy agreed to face her mental—not to mention financial—demons in the dentist's chair. It's only fair that you remain here and study," Anya said.

"It's settled then," Willow said. "Spike can stay here with Dawn while she studies. Spike, you work on our little, uh, guest. I'll go with Anya to find Xander. I'll have to hack into the city plans when we get back." She rolled her eyes. "The city council just re-encrypted them and put up a new firewall at their Web site."

Dawn smiled. "So that should take you—what?—an extra ten minutes."

Willow managed to look simultaneously embarrassed and proud. "Spike will be here in case Xander calls, and he can fill in Giles and Buffy when they get back."

"And are we sure he went to the donut shop?" Dawn asked.

Anya waved a hand at the coffee table. "Look at his note."

Willow picked it up. "It just says he went to get breakfast and that he'd be back by seven."

"No, here, silly," Anya said, pointing at the bottom of the paper.

Willow's face wore a quizzical look. "The hugs and kisses? It's just XOXOX. And then Xander."

"But look at the Os. They're little donuts," Anya said. Everyone bent for a closer look.

"Huh," Willow said. "Yup, definitely donuts."

Anya gave them a smug smile. "You know what a sweet tooth Xander has."

Willow looked wary. "Tooth? No tooth. We have enough teeth today."

"Xander says I'm his favorite sweet in all the world. Though chocolate runs a close second."

"Oh, *please*," Spike said. "Would you just get on with it and go out and find the man? If I have to listen to any more of this I'll go into a diabetic coma."

Willow and Anya practically ran to the donut shop, scanning for any sign of Xander along the way. There were three customers waiting at the donut counter, none of them Xander. Anya knew even as she questioned them that they couldn't have seen Xander, since they had just arrived, but desperation made her try anyway. She pulled out a picture of Xander and showed it around, but all of the customers and the counter girl shook their heads.

The two cops having donuts and coffee in the corner had not seen him either, and seemed spectacularly uninterested. Perhaps, as officers in Sunnydale, they had learned to stay calm, no matter the situation. One of them even had the nerve to chuckle. "Jeez, lady. Do you know how many missing persons reports we get? And your boyfriend's been gone, what, a couple of hours? Gimme a break." He shook his head.

"Okay," Willow said in a reasonable voice, trying to calm the hysteria that seemed to be building in Anya. "He's not here. This is no time to wig out. Where do we look next? Did you try the apartment?"

Anya nodded. "There was no answer. But he could have been taking a shower."

Willow looked at the woman behind the counter. "Do you still have the number my friend gave you when she called this morning?" Willow showed her the picture of Xander again. "Please call if you see him." Then she took Anya's arm and steered her out of the donut shop and down the street.

"That must be it, right?" Anya said, desperately grasping at a simple explanation. They walked faster. "He was sweaty from the fight last night and decided to go home to take a shower."

"Maybe," Willow said, but her voice sounded doubtful.

Anya wracked her mind for a better explanation. "What if he was in the shower and the ants attacked him?" She could hear the ragged edge in her voice. "He doesn't like bugs. He almost got eaten by one."

Their steps quickened and soon they were running again. When they reached the apartment, the door was open and Anya burst through it. In the kitchen, a man was bent over looking at something on the floor. "Xander!" she cried, and threw her arms around him. The man stood up and turned abruptly. Anya screamed. "You're not Xander! Who are you and what have you done with him?"

Willow moved to Anya's side and tried to calm her. The man backed away and pressed himself against the kitchen counter. "I, uh, think his name is Ernie," Willow said, pointing to the name patch sewn onto the man's uniform, right above the picture of a dead roach with a lightning bolt through it. Beneath the picture of the ex-bug were the words Pest-o-Zap.

"The manager let me in," the man explained hurriedly. "She said it would be all right. I ain't seen your husband, lady."

"He . . . he hasn't been here?" Anya was surprised by the man's error, but she found she didn't really want to correct him. "Let's check around anyway," she urged. They made a quick, thorough sweep of the apartment, even looking into cupboards and under furniture, but there was no sign that Xander had been there since the evening before. They returned to the kitchen where Ernie was spraying a mist of liquid onto the floor from a pressurized bottle that hung at his side.

"Make them go away," Anya said, pointing at the ants that were still crawling across the counters and floor. "My . . . Xander doesn't like bugs. Can you get rid of them? Please kill them all."

Ernie wiped a hand across his cheek, leaving a greasy smudge on it. "Sure I can kill them. But this is just a bandage here," he said, pointing to the liquid insecticide. "To really get rid of the problem, you gotta go to the source of the infestation. Could be in the basement, could be in the wall, maybe somewhere outside. May have to look around a bit, but don't worry, I'll find it. And when I do," he gave a little squirt from the bottle of pressurized poison, "they're dead."

"Okay. No Xander here. We move on," Willow told Anya. "Is there . . . is there anyone you can call?"

Anya searched through a kitchen drawer and fished out a piece of paper. "This is a list of some of Xander's coworkers. Perhaps they've seen him."

Willow nodded. "Definitely worth a try."

Twenty frustrating minutes of calls yielded no new clues to Xander's whereabouts. "You think he might have, you know, gone into the sewers or maybe back to Weatherly Park?" Willow asked.

Anya shook her head firmly. "There's no *I* in *team*. Xander wouldn't go there without us—and certainly not without bringing us breakfast first."

"Good point," Willow admitted. "Then I'm guessing there must be some clue along the way between the donut shop and Buffy's house."

"Clues," Anya mused. "Yes, there must be something. All right, let's go." She turned swiftly to the exterminator. "Thank you, Ernie. Please feel free to continue in your genocidal efforts with these insects until you're completely successful."

With that, she and Willow headed back to the Summers home on Revello Drive.

• • •

They walked back to Buffy's house on the opposite side of the street from the one they'd taken on the way to the donut shop. They walked slowly this time, looking at every crack in the sidewalk, every fence in front of every house, each bush, patch of grass, tree, and pile of leaves. Anya saw the familiar pink box first, shoved beneath a bush about three feet away from the sidewalk. With her bandaged hand, she grabbed Willow's wrist and pointed and saw her fellow Scooby swallow hard.

Willow's forehead tensed and her eyes looked uncertain. "It doesn't have to mean anything . . . really, you know, bad. . . ." Her voice trailed off.

The girls knelt together on the grass beside the bush and pulled the box out from underneath. Anya felt something soft beneath her knee and lifted it up to find a piece of smashed cruller.

"Uh-oh," Willow said. She lifted her left hand from the ground and turned it over to show Anya a wooden cross. Holding her breath, Anya flipped open the box. It was empty except for a few smears of icing and red jelly filling and some topping sprinkles. And one perfectly formed, translucent, black-veined wing.

Anger and fear exploded inside Anya like an emotional hand grenade. "It can't be. They can't have Xander. It's not fair."

Willow bit her lip. "The other night—you know, when they attacked Dawn and Tara and me—they tried to carry away a puppy . . . and last night they almost got you." She put a hand on Anya's still-bandaged wrist. "Now it's Xander."

Cold fury surged through Anya's veins, and she felt a thirst for vengeance stronger than any she had felt since becoming human. "We need to find those fairies," she said in a subzero voice. "They have Xander. They need to die."

Chapter Twenty-Three

Buffy and Giles returned to the house just minutes after Willow and Anya had stumbled through the door with the chilling news that Xander had been captured. In spite of her numb tooth and cheek, or perhaps because of it, Buffy suddenly felt ready to take on anything again. She and Giles found Spike, Anya, Willow, and Dawn gathered around the dining-room table, where their captive fairy lay. Willow had her laptop open in front of her, surfing the Web with a look of fierce determination. They had brewed the pot of coffee that Xander had set up, and each of them held a cup, with the exception of Dawn, who had hot chocolate.

Giles leaned back against the wall, holding his glasses in one hand and nibbling on the earpiece, while

Willow and Anya described what they had found in their hunt for Xander.

Buffy paced while she listened. "And there was no other sign of Xander? Torn clothing, maybe?"

Willow's eyebrows scrunched into a forehead frown. "Nothing but the empty donut box. And a cross. Definitely no blood or, you know, bodies or anything."

Giles pursed his lips. "For whatever reason, they've most likely taken Xander to their lair."

Spike got up and went into the kitchen and returned to the head of the dining table with a flyswatter. Dawn picked at a nonexistent speck on the table in front of her. "So if we're sure that the fairies have Xander, how do we find them?"

"Got to get a bit more creative," Spike said.

The five humans and one vampire gathered into a tight semicircle around Lucket.

"So how do we make him talk?" Dawn asked.

Willow gave her an impish smile. "We tie him down and spank him?" When everybody sent her strange looks, she added, "Xander would have understood that. What, doesn't anybody here remember their *Monty Python*?"

"The best part's Arthur and the Black Knight," Spike said. "'What are you going to do, bleed on me?'"

Anya nodded. "Xander and I like to play Castle Anthrax. Have you ever played Castle Anthrax? I'm usually Zoot. 'Oh, wicked, bad, *naughty* Zoot!'"

Giles cleared his throat. "Yes, well, the brilliance of British comedy aside, perhaps we should actually get back to questioning the prisoner."

Buffy nodded. "A wise doctor once told me—okay, it was actually today—that if a problem is bad enough you may have to get to the root of a problem to solve it. We need to figure out where *all* the fairies are."

"Ernie the exterminator said it's important to find the source of the infestation," Anya said, absently rubbing her bandaged wrist.

The fairy growled unconvincingly and crossed its little arms across its tiny chest. Spike picked up the fly-swatter and slapped it against his palm, making sure that the fairy got a good view.

Buffy cut to the chase. "Your friends took one of our friends. We need information."

Anya sat in a chair and pulled it close to the table. "Tell me where my boyfriend is. Where did they take Xander?"

"To his death'd be my guess," the winged creature scoffed in his mini-mafioso voice. "Should be no surprise to you. We're exactly what you made us."

"Wow," Willow said. "Definitely some serious blame issues happening here. But what does Xander have to do with it?"

Lucket hissed. "After we bit the big one, so to speak, Queen Mabyana swore an oath to every fairy in our troop that if we ever bumped into that vengeance demon or the sorceress again, she'd take revenge on them and any of their friends. Send 'em to sleep with the fishes."

"And you already killed the sorceress," Dawn said.

Buffy glanced at Anya. "Sounds like Xander's the worm on the hook."

"Let's get this straight," Spike said. "Xander's being held captive as bait, in order to get to Anya. Oh, that's an original idea, init?"

"These fairies know how to set a trap. We'll have to be careful." Buffy hated stating the obvious. Her mind went into overdrive.

Anya stood, almost knocking her chair over. "We can't just leave Xander there. They'll kill him."

Willow spoke up. "I know this will probably sound stupid, but maybe you could just apologize to the fairies and—"

"You're right," Anya said. "That does sound stupid."

Buffy looked apologetically at her red-haired friend. "I have to agree with Anya, Will. We're a couple of centuries—not to mention countless murders—past the time for apologies."

Anya picked up a toothpick and waved it menacingly in front of the fairy's face. "Where did they take Xander?"

Lucket shrugged. "How would I know? I've been here pinned to this board practically ever since we met in the park last night."

Buffy's hand slammed down on the table next to the fairy and her lips curled back in a dangerous look that was almost a snarl. "Enough with the cute. Just tell us where they would have taken him. Where's Fairy Central?"

The fairy pressed his lips together and crossed his arms over his bare chest.

Willow looked from the silent fairy up to Buffy. "What do you think they'll do if we don't find Xander in time?"

Now Lucket spoke. "I couldn't say for sure, but my guess? They'll probably tear him into a thousand pieces. That would be poetic justice, don'tcha think?"

Dawn gasped. "How could they do that?"

The fairy gave an unpleasant laugh. "One piece at a time."

In the darkness of her secret hideaway, Queen Mabyana preened and fluttered in all her golden splendor in front of her captive. Her henchvamps had tied him to an upright post, so that the Fairy Queen could be certain to command his full attention.

Clearly unimpressed, Xander raised his head to glare at Mabyana. "Nice place you got here. Early military-industrial decorating, if I'm not mistaken."

"Demon lover," the golden queen spat. "Your life is in my hands. You dare to mock us when Anyanka herself brought us to this low estate?"

Xander considered briefly. "Yeah. I pretty much dare."

"We will make her feel the pain of losing what she loves most. With our teeth we will peel your flesh slowly from your living body and make Anyanka watch you die. Then we'll begin tearing her." Queen Mabyana ended with a dramatic flourish of her wings.

Xander gave her a wolfish grin. "All offense intended, but I've faced my share of monsters and demons before, and you guys are a pretty . . . small threat. Untie me and I'll show you exactly *how* small."

Microvamps buzzed around Xander, like plague-carrying mosquitoes. They flew at his eyes, grabbed and pulled out hairs on his neck and head, pricked him with their needle-sharp fangs. He recognized what they were doing: tormenting, torturing, and terrorizing. They didn't intend to kill him.

Not yet, anyway.

"What's the matter?" Xander taunted. "Am I just too much man for you?"

"Silence!" Mabyana snapped.

Fairy vamps swirled around his head making a noise like swarming bees.

He struggled against his bonds. "You know, if you'd bring me a cell phone, I could hook you up with a really good exterminator. Clear this pest problem right up."

The Fairy Queen was appalled at the lack of respect. The insolence. The demon's boyfriend willingly added insult to injury. Did he not understand who she was?

Xander opened his mouth again to speak. Queen Mabyana motioned to two of her henchvamps, who flew forward and quickly inserted a gag of tangled string in the rude human's open mouth and tied it at the back of his head.

The queen looked at the prisoner with horror. Did no one teach these humans manners anymore?

Chapter Twenty-Four

"Tough little bloke, ain'tcha?" Spike said, stroking a black-nailed finger along one of the fairy's gossamer wings. "You important enough to your queenie that she'd swap you for our friend—even trade?"

The fairy's face became stoic. "With payback so close? Not on your life. I'm whatcha might call expendable."

"Well then," Giles said, "perhaps she'd be open to a negotiation of some sort?"

The fairy made a rude noise. "What could you offer that can ever make up for what your pal stole from us?"

"Right. When all else fails, whine about your lot in life," Spike scoffed.

"You," Lucket said, spitting up at Spike. "Okay, maybe your body lost its mortal soul. Big whoop. Still, you got eternal life in exchange. Not a bad deal, as deals go. But us? When the vampire demon infested our troop, we got no profit. No reward. Nothing. We were already immortal. What we had was peaceful, playful, perfect lives—until that demon Anyanka came along. No more romping in the sun for us. Nuh-uh. Now our formerly happy spirits are trapped in these little bodies with the demon that she set loose on us." The fairy's already high-pitched voice grew louder and more shrill with each word.

Giles sighed and bent over the fairy. "Allow us to offer our sincerest condolences."

"Whiny git," Spike muttered.

"But you must see," Giles continued, "that harming our friend will in no way compensate for the years of, er, torment you have endured."

"Besides," Willow said, "Xander is innocent. He never did anything to hurt you."

"Yeah? *We* were innocent once," the fairy said, buzzing with righteous anger, "before the infestation. But your friend wasn't totally innocent. You tried to trap us last night, tried to kill us all."

"Got a point there," Spike said. Then, in a stage whisper he added, "Slayers can be a pain in the ass sometimes."

Buffy growled low in her throat. "You haven't been innocent in almost five hundred years, Lucket. You and your winged buds are the ones that started killing people in Sunnydale. We were only trying to stop you."

Willow spoke, "Still with the blame issues. This

isn't how we're going get Xander back."

"Tell us where your troop is hiding," Anya demanded, banging her hand on the table. Her bandaged hand. She winced.

The fairy snarled. His face became lumpy and misshapen, his wings sprouted black veins. "I'd never rat on my queen."

"Really?" Spike said with some interest. Before anyone could stop him, he slipped a finger beneath Lucket's upper right wing and folded it in half. It broke with an audible crunch. The minivamp shrieked and yowled and bared its fangs at them.

Willow gasped.

Too late, Buffy yanked Spike's hand away from the microprisoner.

Dawn stared in shock at the injured fairy and said, "Cool."

Spike glanced up at Giles. "Don't tell me you never did this sort of thing when you were a boy. To a butterfly or a cockroach?"

Giles looked offended. "Why, no. Never."

"Bloody figures," Spike said.

Buffy's mind quickly latched on to a line of reasoning that the little monster would understand. She nudged Spike aside. "Okay, back off a minute." She set her elbows on the table and leaned toward Lucket, squelched her anger, and forced herself to sound upbeat and reasonable. "You wouldn't actually be betraying your queen, you know. She's really setting a trap, with Xander starring in the role of bait. Queen Mabyana needs us to walk into it."

"Indeed," Giles agreed. "You'd be doing her a

great service by directing us to her."

"So, we're willing to stroll right into the trap. No strings. What more could your queen want?" Buffy put her arm around Anya's shoulder. "And I personally guarantee Anya will head straight for the cheese."

"Yes," Anya said. "Cheese. I need it. I need it back now."

Lucket fluttered his wings and seemed to think about this, then relaxed. The wings, including the broken one, returned to gossamer clarity and the face relaxed into the smooth beauty of a fairy once again. "I can't tell you how to get there," the lavender-clad fairy said, "but I could lead you."

"Right, then. We'll just let you fly straight out the door into the sunlight, shall we?" Spike said. He picked up the foam board and walked toward the curtained window.

"Stop." Buffy put her hands on her hips while badcop Spike put the thin foam slab back on the table. "Just describe it, Lucket. We'll take it from there."

"Fairies usually live in hills," Anya said. "Do you live in a hill?"

The fairy's face grew dreamy as if he were thinking of a beautiful, far-away place. "Yeah. Under woodlands and grass. Beautiful. It's kinda like an oasis in the middle of a bunch of black and gray stone."

"An oasis in Sunnydale?" Dawn asked.

"Woodlands and grasses," Willow said. "That's probably a park."

"Well, there's that small hill in Weatherly Park

with the sealed up door," Buffy said, "but there's no way in. Not even a fairy could get in there."

"No, no. Yes there is," Willow said. "Buffy, I did some research while you were at the dentist. According to the city plans, that was once a civil-defense bomb shelter, built during the Cold War by the city council." She shrugged. "I guess they thought they could hide there if there was a nuclear attack. Anyway, once the Cold War ended, they took out all the supplies and the gardeners were using it as an equipment shed. But in 1991 there was some sort of accident. Kids were playing hide-and-seek. One of them got trapped down there and almost died. The parents sued the city. It was a whole big thing. So the city council decided to seal up the entrance from above."

"Thanks, Will," Buffy said. "So we know where the fairies aren't. I take it this is all leading somewhere?"

Willow smiled her I-know-a-secret smile and said, "I said it was sealed up from *above*."

"Then there's another entrance?" Buffy asked.

Willow tilted her head noncommittally from side to side. "Not so much an entrance as an opening," she said.

Recognition lit Spike's face. "From the sewers. Pretty sure I know the spot. I can take you there. Not far from where I found that homeless bloke."

"What are we waiting for?" Willow said.

Anya looked worried but determined. "We need to get Xander back before, before . . ."

"Before anyone else gets hurt?" Willow asked.

"We need to leave immediately," Anya said, flexing her injured hand as if spoiling for a fight.

"No," Buffy said firmly. "We'll leave soon, but this time we need to go in with the right weapons. I don't plan to get whipped again by a bunch of fairies."

Chapter Twenty-Five

With Xander in imminent danger of becoming a steaming pile of Xander bits, there was no time to lose. Who knew? By now some helpless homeless person might already have become the fairy vamps' next meal. One way or another, they had to be stopped.

The Scooby gang had seen some painful changes over the years, but their basic mission had always stayed simple, as simple as the title of a Godzilla movie: *Destroy All Monsters,* with monsters being defined as any nonhuman entity with a tendency to harm and/or kill humans. The fairy vamps had already killed at least three residents of Sunnydale. That alone qualified them to become citizens of dustville as far as the Slayerettes were concerned. And when friends or family were threatened, their desire to kill the offending monsters ratcheted to an entirely new level. The Scoobies went into full-on Rambo mode.

"What we require for this battle is thoroughness and creativity," Giles instructed.

"On it," Buffy said, pushing through the doorway to the kitchen where she began opening cupboards and drawers, looking for anything that could beef up their arsenal. The rest of the gang quickly followed her in and began searching as well.

Buffy rummaged under the kitchen sink and said, "A-ha!" She straightened, holding up a squirt bottle of blue liquid.

Giles blinked several times. "You intend to poison them with glass cleaner?"

"Hardly," Buffy said.

Anya looked misty-eyed. "That's the same kind of cleaner Xander used to kill our ants."

Buffy unscrewed the spray top of the bottle and dumped the blue liquid into a plastic bowl on the counter. "Dawn, I need you to find that butterfly net Dad got you when you were ten. Then bring all the holy water you can find in my room." Dawn ran for the stairs.

"I understand." Anya gave a nod of recognition. "You're making insecticide—or fairicide, in this case, I guess. I approve."

Spike turned from where he was looking through an upper cupboard. "Twisted. I like the way you think."

"Less talk," Buffy said, "more weapons."

From a drawer, Giles pulled a box of sturdy deli toothpicks, the kind topped with a colorful plastic frill.

"I suppose these will still have to do for close-up work," he said. He distributed a small handful to each member of the team. "Remember, if you've got one stunned or immobilized, go for the kill."

Dawn dashed back into the room carrying holy water, several crosses, and the butterfly net. She put down all but one of the crosses and slid the toothpicks Giles had given her into a pocket of her pants. "Crosses should still work, shouldn't they? They burn the vampires."

"Definitely," Willow said. "Ooh, look," she said, holding up something she pulled from a drawer. "Pipe cleaners." When everyone stared blankly at her, she said, "You know, in case we need to take any more captives?"

"Speaking of," Spike said, "what are we planning to do with Tom Thumb in there?" He indicated the dining room with a jerk of his head.

"Better leave him here," Buffy said. "If anything goes wrong, we may still need to pump him for information."

Spike made a noise of disgust and picked something out of the cupboard beside the stove with a pair of tongs and quickly handed it off to Giles. "Garlic powder," he explained. "Bit of seasoning for the little wingies."

"What's this?" Anya asked, holding up a small canister with a nozzle on it.

"Butane torch," Buffy said, looking down somberly at the floor.

Dawn picked up the cylinder. "It was Mom's. She

took a cooking class once. She used this to make little crème brûlées."

"Fire is good," Anya said. "It kills vampires. And it's light enough to hold in my hurt hand. I'll use this."

"Any other suggestions?" Giles asked.

"Yeah, how about body armor?" Dawn said.

Giles raised his eyebrows. "That's actually not such a silly idea. We should all be in full protective gear."

"Everyone but Spike. He's not in much danger," Dawn said.

Spike used strapping tape to attach toothpicks to the fingertips of his left hand. "Even so, Nibblet, this'll be a rough fight for me."

"Why?" Dawn challenged.

He gave a sardonic smile. "Because, the stakes are so small."

Pouring holy water into the spray bottle, Buffy growled. "Not too small to put you out of our misery if all you can do is make jokes. Dawn, find me another squirt bottle." She screwed the top back on the bottle. "Everyone except Spike make sure you're in full protective clothing: long sleeves, high necks, gloves, jackets, and leather if you've got 'em."

"I don't think we have enough weapons," Dawn said, handing Buffy another small pump sprayer. She looked at Anya. "Didn't you say there could be a thousand fairies? We can't kill a thousand of these things one by one."

Anya seemed impatient at the delay. "We can bring Xander's Slayomatic. Of course, we'll still only slaughter five or so at a time, but—"

"What about sunlight?" Giles asked. "Or fire?"

Willow shook her head and pulled on a jacket. "From what I saw in the city plans, their hideout is too far underground. I mean, it was built to protect people from nukes and radiation. Walls are solid concrete lined with lead. Plus, when they sealed the entrance, they pretty much stripped out all the perishable supplies and most of the furniture."

Buffy sighed. "So I'm guessing the bonfire option is out too. Unless . . ." She checked some cupboards and found several more butane canisters and a bottle of lighter fluid. Definitely the beginnings of a lethal weapon. "Will, do you think there's anything you could add magickwise to—"

"You can't ask her to do the teleportation spell," Giles warned. "Too dangerous."

"I won't need to," Willow said. "Anyway, we're not trying to push them away from us. But there may be something I can do if I could get a few supplies from the Magic Box."

"Of course," Giles said. "Perhaps we'll find additional useful implements there. Spike, you take the tunnels. We'll meet you at the shop. The rest of you can come with me in the car."

Minutes later they were at the Magic Box, where a quick search yielded several more useful items. Spike found a South American blowgun with handfuls of tiny wooden darts. Anya gathered more garlic powder while Willow collected some ingredients and put them in a bag. Buffy selected an antique penknife. Giles picked up a heavy-duty flashlight of the sort that is equally useful as a cudgel once the batteries are drained.

Buffy handed Dawn a candle in a ceramic pot and then took a large wooden torch like those used in medieval-castle movies. They all went down to the basement of the Magic Box to the mouth of the sewer tunnel Spike had used to get there. Buffy, concerned for her little sister, pulled Dawn's turtleneck a bit higher and buttoned two more buttons on her sister's jacket.

"Come on then, Mother Hen. Time's a-wastin'," Spike said.

"Stay out of the main fighting," Buffy warned Dawn. Then to Spike she said, "Lay off, McDuff. We're ready."

"Yeah," Willow said. "Let's go kick some fairy butt."

Chapter Twenty-Six

Buffy could think of plenty of things she'd rather be doing than following Spike through the sewers of Sunnydale preparing to fight a mosh pit full of mini enemies. Being back in the dentist's chair having a root canal, for example, sounded like lots more fun.

Spike's leather duster billowed out behind him like the flapping wings of some dark bird of prey. The toothpicks attached to his left hand might have been talons. With grim looks on their faces, Anya and Buffy paced him. Dawn, Willow, and Giles brought up the rear, carrying a bright flashlight. Most of them held toothpicks in their mouths as a precaution. As Spike had pointed out, you never knew whether the treacherous flying buggers might have set up an ambush.

Although they moved quickly through the tunnels, as quiet as museum curators wearing felt slippers, to

Buffy it felt as if they were walking in slow motion. Her nerves were wound tighter than an Egyptian mummy's wrappings. This was no mere bust-and-dust operation. It was also a rescue and quite possibly a war. Precision would be more important than ever before.

Even the liveliest of alleyway brawls with vampires could not begin to compare with the sheer nerve-wrackingness of facing down hundreds of magickal, demon-infested, dragonfly-sized bloodsuckers. Homicidal hummingbirds, furious fairies, vengeful vamps—all of whom wanted to terminate one or more of the Slayerettes with extreme prejudice. Buffy gritted her teeth at the thought. One nice surprise there: no pain in her teeth.

"Gettin' close now," Spike whispered as they turned a corner. Buffy's muscles tensed.

The sewer reeked and the floor was slippery. Suddenly, as if out of nowhere, something dark and frantic fluttered up from the floor and into their faces. Buffy started to lash out at it.

"Wait, it's"—Willow gave a nervous laugh— "just a pigeon."

Buffy lowered her hand and squinted in the dimness and saw that Willow was right. The startled pigeon flew up to ceiling level and squeezed out through a storm drain into the sunlight above.

"Isn't it kind of weird for a bird—," Dawn began.

Buffy took the toothpick from her mouth and held up a hand for silence. "Hate to interrupt such a perfect John Woo moment, but listen."

They all heard it, a muffled yell repeated every ten seconds or so. Giles straightened his glasses. "I believe that's—"

"Xander!" Anya said.

They all ran the final twenty feet to where a three foot square opening yawned at chest level in the sewer wall. On the floor beneath the hole, a heavy, square lead plate leaned against the curved wall.

"You sure it's not an air duct?" Dawn asked. "That's really the entrance?"

Willow gave a kind of shrug with her eyebrows. "The one and only. Your tax dollars at work."

Again, a muffled yell came, from the direction of the opening this time, and louder than before. Buffy turned away from the hole and started issuing orders. "Spike will take point, and I'll go in after. Giles, I need you to be Boost Guy. Help Anya, Willow, and Dawn get into the hole, then bring up the rear so—"

"Stop her," Giles said.

Buffy whipped back toward the opening only to find that Anya, holding the Slayomatic in her injured hand, had already scrambled inside and was crawling through the concrete tunnel.

"Bloody 'ell," Spike said, and heaved himself in after her.

Tucking the unlit wooden torch under one arm, Buffy launched herself into the opening. She thought of telling Spike to hold Anya back, but it was too late. The short tunnel came to an end, and Buffy tumbled out a foot above floor level into a gigantic room, dimly lit by emergency lamps. Spike was helping Anya to her feet, and Buffy sprang up to an alert fighting stance.

"Take this." Anya shoved the Slayomatic into Spike's hands and looked around to get her bearings. Willow, Dawn, and Giles made their way into the room and stood by Spike.

The room looked almost completely empty at first. Against the wall stood rows of tri-level bunk beds without mattresses. The bunks were made of the same gray-enameled government-issue metal as the empty supply shelves and the old battered desk on the far wall. The chamber was twice as large as the basketball court at Sunnydale High had been. The surprisingly chilly air smelled of dust and mold . . . and death.

Across the room Xander was lashed upright to the pole of one of the bunk beds, wrapped in uneven light-colored filaments that made him look like an inept silkworm trying to spin a cocoon. His head moved slightly and he let out a groan. He looked up, saw his friends, and tried to shout something around the gag that bound his mouth.

Anya and Buffy ran toward him. Xander shook his head and frantically darted his eyes in the direction of the ceiling several times. Buffy looked up and saw that the ceiling seemed to be carpeted with something dark. Something that moved. "Giles?" Buffy said. Giles held up his flashlight and played it across the upper portion of the shelter to get a better look.

Hundreds of miniature vampires dangled upside down like tiny bats from the ceiling.

"You tramp," Anya said, shocking Buffy anew. "Get off of him."

Buffy looked back at Xander and saw a golden-haired fairy in a sheer green dress appear. The fairy crawled up the back of Xander's head to the top and now stood in his brown hair, surrounded by a confident golden aura. "Queen Bee, I presume?" Buffy quipped.

Mabyana lifted a delicate hand and waved it high in the air. In unison, the creatures overhead released their hold on the ceiling and plummeted like black rain toward the floor. The Scoobies were in the trap and the battle had begun.

Chapter Twenty-Seven

Sounds of heated combat erupted everywhere in the room, but Anya's eyes were glued to Xander. Surprise number one was that the descending hordes of vampire fairies avoided Xander and Anya completely. They attacked everyone else, though, and drove Buffy backward from Xander by sheer force. Anya threw herself toward him, ignoring the pain in her wrist and the two minivamps in her boyfriend's hair, and began to tear at the tangle of string that bound him.

Deluged by fairies, Buffy tossed down the wooden torch, dropped into a backward roll, bounced up, and did a tight spin, throwing off most of the flittering vamps that had clung to her clothing. She let out a dizzying spate of precise punches and kicks as she whirled. Without pausing, Buffy dug into her pocket and found the penknife there. "Anya," she called, and threw the knife toward the girl. "Cut Xander loose. We'll hold them off."

Anya tried to catch the knife with her bandaged hand and missed. The knife clattered to the floor. She spent precious seconds fumbling around for it on the dusty linoleum. Xander shook his head and tried frantically to say something around his gag. "Got it," Anya said, finding the small knife and flipping open the blade. There were still only two fairies on Xander: the queen and one of her henchvamps, which had crawled down Xander's face and was trying to bite into the artery at his temple.

Xander shook his head, eyes wide with panic. He shouted something that sounded something like, "Eck, eck."

With her free hand, Anya slapped the copper-colored fairy. It dodged out of the way and Anya's hand connected with Xander's cheek with a loud smack. "Eck!" Xander yelled again, darting his eyes upward as he had before.

Anya looked up to see Queen Mab repeatedly sinking her fangs into Xander's scalp, not a deadly act but one surely meant to taunt Anya. The ex-demon decided to teach the Fairy Queen a lesson—one that she wouldn't live long enough to forget. Pulling the butane canister from her jacket pocket, Anya lit the chef's torch.

Xander's wide eyes filled with panic, and he ducked as Anya brought the small torch up toward Queen Mab. The microqueen of the damned pushed off from Xander's scalp and flitted up toward the ceiling.

Xander's head snapped up again and his eyes pleaded with Anya. "Eck!"

Anya turned off the chef's torch, slid it back into her pocket. Believing she understood what he was saying, Anya nodded. "Yes, I want sex too, but we'll have to get you out of here first." She switched the penknife to her right hand cut through the gag of rope and shredded rags. She yanked the gag away and kissed Xander on the mouth.

He returned her kiss for a split second, then jerked his head back and said, "*Desk,* not sex. Up there." She looked up.

Above them, suspended by a hodge-podge of string, shredded cloth, and rope was an enormous army-style metal desk that must have weighed three hundred pounds. When they entered the room, it had been hidden from view by clusters of dark fairy vamps, but now only a few of the creatures clung to the supporting strands, nibbling on them. Rope and string frayed, and the desk swung precariously. There was no time to think. Anya sliced through the bonds that held Xander to the upright post of the triple bunk, grabbed him, and dove onto the naked metal springs of the bottom bunk.

Just in time.

The rope holding the desk gave way and the metal behemoth swung downward. Two of the desk's steel legs hit the top bunk, catching there and collapsing the bed to its second level. The main body of the desk and the other two legs arced downward like a two-ton wrecking ball, smashed into the side of the bunk, and then clanged to the floor exactly where Xander and Anya had been standing. Drawers popped open, and a few dozen pristine No. 2 pencils flew out and scattered on the floor.

Xander and Anya lay panting for a moment. "We almost got hit by a desk," he said.

"It wouldn't have been the first time," Anya said.

"Knew you missed me," Xander quipped, "but I didn't think you'd try to get me into bed this fast."

Metal screeched above them. Anya grabbed Xander and rolled off the bunk out onto the floor. The upper two bunks collapsed onto the lower one.

"'Course," Xander said, "always a woman's prerogative to change her mind. And, not that I mind you being on top—"

Anya pressed her mouth to his and kissed him, longer this time. "You're sweet."

Xander grinned. "Probably just the donuts. But maybe you could untie me? I'm feeling a little pinned down here."

Anya finished cutting Xander free from his tangled cocoon. Buffy paused in her fighting to help Xander to his feet. It felt good to be free again.

Back at Buffy's house, Lucket tried to break free. Ignoring the pain in his gut, he grabbed at the wooden stake that held him down. He twisted and rocked it back and forth. He pulled hard with his deceptively strong arms. Three of his wings pushed him upward, but the fourth, the broken one, refused to respond. The wing might heal, given time. If he managed to escape. Other fairies might have given up, but as long as he was alive, he had a duty to help his queen, the enchanting Mabyana.

He clamped his miniature perfect teeth together and yanked at the wooden toothpick again and again. He braced his feet beneath him and pushed up, straining with feet, thighs, wings, and arms. Finally the small wooden spear came free in his hands. Lucket staggered to his feet, struggling to gather his strength, and flung the piece of wood far away. Forcing himself to fly in spite of his broken wing, Lucket made a circuit of the room in what looked like a drunken flutter, avoiding the direct sunlight that streamed in through the window.

At last he saw his chance. The kitchen sink was still in shade. He landed on the kitchen counter, crawled beneath the shaft of sunlight, and threw himself down the drain. With any luck, he would soon see his queen.

Back in the storm shelter, pandemonium reigned. That, and holy water. With his spray bottle set to mist, Giles shot clouds of acid spray into the air that melted the delicate wings of the vampettes, who plummeted to the linoleum.

"There are too many of them." Buffy picked up the wooden torch, lit it, waved it, and fried a few incoming.

Willow took a handful of powder from a pouch tied to her belt loop. She threw the powder high into the air and muttered a few words in Latin, wishing that Tara were here beside her, instead of tutoring David Wilson.

"What was that? What did you do?" Anya asked.

Buffy took the toothpick from her mouth and staked a minivamp that was doing a kamikaze straight toward her face. It burst into a cloud of glittering dust, mere inches from her green eyes. "Will that disable them, Will?"

"Not permanently," Willow said, watching the spell take effect. Suddenly every fairy the powder had touched, probably two hundred in all, went into microscopic convulsions accompanied by tiny sharp squeaking sounds. With each convulsion, the fairies twirled or spun end-over-end.

"What the—," Xander began.

"A sneezing spell," Willow explained. "It'll keep some of them busy for a while so they can't all attack at once."

Over near the entrance, Dawn had set her candle down and was using her butterfly net to scoop handfuls of non-allergic fairies from the air. She misted the net with holy water, and when she swung the net down with ten or so fairies in it, she quickly upended it over the potted candle, and shook. Three fairies burned in the candle flame. The rest ran frantically around inside a circle of garlic powder Dawn had sprinkled around the candle.

"Good work, Nibblet," Spike said.

"Shake and bake, just like Mom taught me," she said, pointing at the badly singed microvamps on the floor. Spike bent down and precision staked them with the toothpicks on his fingertips, careful not to touch the garlic powder.

Giles sprayed more holy water into the air and another handful of disabled fairies dropped to the floor. Several enraged wingless vamps threw themselves at his feet and crawled up his pant legs.

Suddenly Spike was there with the Slayomatic. He swung it lightly downward, killing six of the fairies with one blow. Giles shook his foot, and three fairies lost their grip and slid out of his pants leg. Spike tapped the Slayomatic again across the floor and across Giles's shoes. Giles, still being attacked from above, sprayed again. Spike rolled away, shouting colorful curses. "Hello? Vampire here. *Not* the enemy," he said, putting a hand up to his badly burned cheek. "Watch who you're shooting with that stuff."

"Terribly sorry," Giles said. "Thanks for the assist."

In pain and frustration, Spike swung the Slayomatic overhead, dusting three minivamps in midair.

Anya and Xander fought their way over to the others. Buffy executed a flying kick that sent several flying vamps . . . well . . . flying, and stopped beside them, breathing hard. Several fairies approached from above, carrying a broken chunk of cinderblock, ready to drop it on Anya's head.

"Look out!" Willow yelled.

Chapter Twenty-Eight

Buffy reacted on sheer instinct. She dropped her torch. "Duck," she snapped, bounding to the top of the nearest bunk bed, pushing off and nailing the cinderblock-carrying vamps with a flying kick three feet above Anya's head. Buffy's legs caught her with a shock-absorber landing just on the other side of Xander, and she bounced back to her feet, shaking her finger in the air. "*Bad* fairies."

"Okay, fill me in," Xander said. He lashed a fist upward at a cluster of approaching wingies. "What are the big guns?"

"Spike has a blowgun," Anya said, shaking a glowing aqua fairy from her head. Spike slid the Slayomatic across the floor toward Xander, and pulled out the blowgun.

"No, no, no, no," Xander said, scooping up the

Slayomatic. "I mean the grand finale. The big beef. How do we take these little suckers out permanently? You know, micro-Armageddon."

Buffy absently delivered a punch and then a roundhouse kick to another batch of approaching fairies. "Plan. Right. It involves fire."

Xander's eyes narrowed. "You sure you have a plan? A.k.a., Slayerettes win, vampettes lose?"

"We brought weapons. We rescued you." Anya hugged Xander. A trio of henchvamps flew in overhead.

Xander swept the Slayomatic upward and took out one of them. "Maybe it's just me, but I'd be a bit cautious about that last assumption there."

"Hate to interrupt your ladies' tea," Spike called from across the room, staking a fairy vamp in the air with one fingertip, "but we've got a war on here."

Anya pulled out her chef's torch again. Xander hefted the Slayomatic. Buffy sprang back into action—literally. She picked up her wooden torch, swung herself to the top bunk of the row of beds that lined one wall, held the torch high in the air, and sizzled a cluster of fairies that hovered twelve feet above the floor. She bounced, testing the springs. The metal coils held firm and gave a satisfying creak. She jumped high and sizzled every flying vamp she could reach with her torch. When her feet touched back down on the springs, she bounced up into a forward somersault and landed on the next bunk over.

On the floor Xander flailed with the Slayomatic, taking out five or so flying vamps with each pass.

"Gee, at this rate, Sunnydale should be safe from microvamps in, oh, a year or two."

Willow flung a handful of garlic powder into the air, repelling the fairies around her who had not already sneezed themselves out of the line of fire. The garlic-flavored vamps dropped to the floor, coughing and retching, and Willow knelt beside them. She took the pipe cleaners from her pocket, but saw no efficient way to make use of them. She secured a couple of toothpicks to her fingertips with the fuzzy wires and began picking off the lethal pests. "They're cute," she said, pouting slightly at the necessity of having to kill the precious miniatures.

"Cute?" Buffy echoed. She had a rhythm going now across the bunk beds. Bounce, swing, sizzle, bounce, somersault to new bed, bounce, swing, sizzle.

"Yeah," Willow said. She held up a cross as twenty bad fairies darted toward her. "You know, in an evil, ugly sort of way. And—and numerous. Let's not forget numerous." Most of the fairies flew away from the crucifix. Some of them simply swerved around it. "Sorry." She batted two of them out of the air with the cross and was rewarded with a satisfying sizzle as they dispersed in a crackle of scintillating dust. "Ooh. Pretty."

"Running out of ammunition," Giles reported. A tiny vampire landed on his turtleneck collar and bit the bare skin just above it. "Blast," he said, but before he could bring a hand up to swat at it, the microvamp dissolved into a puff of ash. Giles glanced to his side and saw Spike fifteen feet away, reloading his blowgun near the entrance beside Dawn.

Dawn swept her holy-water-dampened butterfly net through the air again and caught several flying monsters. "Is this what they mean by fly-fishing?" she wondered aloud.

"Thank you, Spike," Giles said.

"Don't mention it," said Spike. "No, really, I mean it. Don't."

"Yes, well, mind you don't let any get away," Giles said.

Spike looked down at the entry tunnel just as something small and glowing darted past him. *Into* the room. A silver-haired sprite with a broken wing and lavender clothing. "Bugger all," Spike said. "Knew I should have offed that fairy when I had the chance."

"It's Lucket," Dawn said, recognizing the tink.

Anya crawled along the floor with her tiny chef's torch, dusting any minivamps that had been grounded by stunning blows or holy water. A line of them stretched to the wall of the bomb shelter, reminding her of a trail of oversized nightmare insects. She burned and staked and burned again. "Much more satisfying than chasing ants." As she worked her way to the corner by the wall, Anya suddenly found herself face-to-face with Queen Mab and two of the queen's vampy minions.

Anya bared her teeth in a feral, animal expression of anger. "You tried to kill my Xander. I'll rip your wings off. Then you'll die." She rushed forward, chef's torch held high. Anya's small fuel canister chose that moment to run out of butane. The torch sputtered out.

At a sign from the queen, a swarm of henchvamps

dove in and took hold of Anya's hair and clothing. Queen Mab said one word: "Anyanka."

Anya shook her head. "No, not Anyanka. Just Anya. I'm not a demon anymore. What do you want from me?"

Queen Mab fluttered forward till she almost touched Anya's nose. "Vengeance," she hissed. "You, of all people, should understand that."

Countless microvamps crawled onto any exposed piece of Anya's flesh and bit down.

Anya tried to shake them off. "I was a demon. I was doing my job. That was five hundred years ago. Get over it."

"So Anyanka no longer has any powers. That should make this easy then," Mab said, pulsating with golden light. "And all the more delicious."

Xander appeared behind Anya. "Nobody's gonna go all *Lord of the Flies* on my girlfriend." He started pulling flitter critters off of Anya's fang-bitten flesh.

Buffy did an aerial flip with a half twist and landed beside Xander. Willow and Giles appeared at Xander's other side. "*This* is the Queen Bee?" Buffy said in disbelief.

"Leave Anya alone or I'll throw a teleportation spell at you so hard it'll smash you and your friends into a paste against that wall," Willow said, brandishing her crucifix for good measure.

"She can do it," Giles said in a mild tone.

"You're right," Anya said to Mab. "I don't have any *powers,* but I do have friends."

The outraged queen spun like some sort of dervish insect and arrowed up toward the ceiling, followed by her miniature honor guard. A streak of lavender joined them.

"Way to go, Will," Xander said, slapping the back of the Slayomatic against his palm. "Very high intimidation factor."

Buffy rested her hands on her hips. "I'd give it a five point eight for technical merit."

"You . . ."—Willow took a quick breath— "you think they might want to just go away now?"

"They should do," Spike said from his post guarding the entrance. "I reckon we've killed about half their lot."

"Hmm," Xander said. "Maybe we won't need that grand finale after all."

"Buffy!" Dawn shrieked.

Buffy looked up to see several hundred glowing microvamps hurtling toward them with a menacing drone. She held her torch high. "Looks like the fat lady still has to sing. Everybody give me your butane canisters, lighter fluid, matches, anything combustible, and get out as fast as you can. I'll meet you in the sewer tunnel."

The fairies were almost upon them as the Scoobies piled their flammables at Buffy's feet. Anya collected the wooden pencils that had fallen out of the dropped desk. Xander gathered the string and cloth that the fairies had used to tie him up and suspend the desk from the ceiling. Dawn tossed her potted candle to her sister, who caught it one-handed. Giles added some matches and toothpicks, then threw a pocket handkerchief onto the mound.

Willow dropped the remaining pipe cleaners and toothpicks to the mix, waved her hand over the bonfire-to-be, and whispered, "As moth to flame, so ends this game." She glanced at Buffy. "That should attract them, but it won't last for long."

Buffy's mouth was set in a grim line. "If it draws the tinks down here, that's all I need."

All the holy water was gone now, and the Slay-erettes started to fight their way out.

"Some help here," Dawn called, trying to fight off a small batch of commando vamps that had gone straight for her.

"I'm on it, Nibblet," Spike said, moving to help her.

Xander swung the Slayomatic, clearing a path toward the exit. Buffy twirled the flaming torch in circles overhead while she knelt on the floor, building her pile of pint-sized explosives. She arranged the butane canisters and sprinkled the matches, pencils, and toothpicks around them. Next, Buffy smashed the pot with its liquefied candle wax on the floor, then opened a small bottle of lighter fluid and squirted it in a wide puddle for good measure. She thought she remembered that linoleum would burn at high enough temperatures. She certainly hoped so. She glanced toward the entrance tunnel and saw that only Spike remained in the room. "Go now!" she yelled. He didn't wait to be told a second time.

Buffy pushed to her feet and, with a final swing of the torch to clear her way, took three running steps toward the exit. She turned and lobbed the torch at the mound of combustibles, then threw herself into the short tunnel that led to the sewers. The room lit up behind her as Buffy wriggled out. Giles and Xander grabbed her arms as soon as she was close enough and pulled her out into the tunnel.

"Help me," Buffy said, grabbing the lead cover plate that leaned against the wall beneath the hole she'd just climbed out of. She and Giles took one side, Xander and Spike took the other, and they lifted it up and slammed it into place.

A shockwave punched at the metal plate from the inside, but they held it firmly closed. They stood panting for a long while, listening for any signs that the micromenaces were still trying to get out. Nothing. Finally they began the slow walk through the sewers back toward the Magic Box.

"Yay, us?" Willow said.

Buffy sighed. Some things went completely against the laws of nature. Fairies should never have become vampires. She did not feel happy or triumphant. "Well, at least we stopped them."

"Not entirely, love," Spike said.

"What do you mean?"

Spike stopped, touched a thumb to the center of his forehead at eyebrow level, and closed his eyes, as if trying to forget something unpleasant. "Some of the buggers got away," he said.

"They *what?*" Buffy demanded.

"Escaped," Dawn said, twisting her fingers into a

knot. "While Spike was helping me. Lucket and the Fairy Queen and maybe ten others kind of did an end run."

Queen Mab huddled with Lucket and her few remaining fairies in a dank corner of the sewers where sunlight never reached. At her order, all of their colorful glows had been extinguished. She could not risk being seen. Tiny sparkling tears flowed from her leaf-green eyes. They would hide here until nighttime and then fly up and out of the sewer and away from the Hellmouth.

Perhaps someday they would find a way to increase their strength and return to Sunnydale. Perhaps someday Queen Mab would find a way to take her vengeance on the despised Anyanka.

Chapter Twenty-Nine

Spending the weekend ridding Sunnydale of fangy nuisances had taken up a lot of time, and Buffy and friends found themselves playing catch-up on the details of everyday life for the next few days. So it was Wednesday evening before schedules cooperated and the friends all managed to meet again at the Magic Box.

Anya and Dawn sat on stools at the checkout counter while Anya, her hand now mostly healed, entered rows of neat numbers in a ledger. Giles roamed the shop, straightening the merchandise and commenting occasionally to Anya about items that were low or out of stock. Willow brewed some tea at the side table against one wall while Xander, still wearing his work clothes, lounged across from Tara at the conference table. Buffy, glistening with sweat and wearing a tight white tank top and gray sweat pants, stood near the conference table stretching and cooling down after her workout in the back room. Most of them looked as if they were recovering from a mild case of chicken pox.

"So, Dawnie," Willow said, pouring steaming tea from a ceramic pot into two stoneware mugs, "how did the test go? You know, with the colonies and the dates and all."

Dawn rolled her eyes and gave a noncommittal shrug. "I got the test back today."

Buffy rolled up to a standing position from a touch-the-floor stretch and looked expectantly at her sister. "And?"

Dawn's face dimpled into a smile. "A-minus." She stood and made a little bow.

The jingling of the shop bell was all but covered up by a combination of applause, whistles, and way-to-go comments. With a smirk, Spike ambled down the wide shallow stairs toward the conference table. "Always nice to know I'm appreciated." He hooked a chair from the table with his foot, spun it around, and sat. Without even looking, one of his hands reached up to grab a mug from Willow as she walked past him. He took a deep gulp. "Thanks, pet."

"Hey," Willow said, plunking the other mug down in front of Tara, who thanked her quietly. Willow's brows drew together as she looked at Spike. "That was my . . . You can't just . . ." Her expression grew resigned. "You, uh, need any more sugar with that?"

She walked back to the sideboard to pour another mug of tea.

"Nah." Spike drew a flask from the inside pocket of his jacket, unscrewed the cap, and poured a liberal amount into the mug. "I got it."

"Dawn received an A-minus on her history exam," Anya told Spike. "Giles and I make excellent teachers. Willow and Tara helped as well." She looked at Tara. "Was your tutoring on Sunday equally successful?"

Nonplussed, Tara smoothed a strand of blond hair behind her ear. "I, well, yes. David is very smart. He really knew the material already; he just needed someone to help him go over everything and drill him on the facts."

"Ah, drilling." Xander folded his hands behind his head and leaned back farther in his chair. "That brings us to Buffy. How is our dental patient?"

Buffy raised her hands and tapped herself on either cheek in a *look-Mom-no-pain* sort of gesture and then smiled. "Good as new."

Giles cleared his throat. "You know, Buffy, you needn't keep such things from us." He realphabetized several books on herbology that had gotten out of order. "We're your friends. Your family. We have resources, and you needn't suffer in silence."

"Yup." Willow took a sip from the mug in her hand and sat down beside Tara. "We'd prefer the tooth, the whole tooth, and nothing but the . . ." Her voice trailed off when she caught her friends' pained glances. "Anyone else want some tea?"

Buffy quickly stepped in. "Xander, what's the sitch with the pest problem?"

Xander got his square-jawed military look on his face. "Sir, I'm happy to report that the insurgency has been squashed, sir." He gave a satisfied grin. "Yup, I am feeling mighty gruntled."

"No more little buggies?" Willow asked.

Xander shook his head. "They have succumbed to the rule of law. And speaking of the law, how did your day in court go, Giles?"

"Smooth move, Segue Man," Buffy complimented.

Giles took off his glasses and swept his hazel eyes across them all. "Well, as it turns out, the judge is a woman of great discretion and understanding. And as luck would have it, we share a common interest in medieval religious artifacts. We had a fascinating discussion of the—"

"Giles," Buffy broke in. "The ticket?"

"Oh, yes." Giles blinked and slid his glasses back on. "Dismissed it out of hand. Case closed."

"Our own Erin Brockovich." Anya beamed proudly at him. "You have great courage and a finely honed sense of justice." She closed her ledger book. "May I have a raise?"

"Well, I, er . . ." Giles straightened an arrangement of healing crystals. "Fifty cents an hour?"

"A dollar," Anya said in a firm voice.

Giles pursed his lips. "Seventy-five cents and not a penny more."

"Done." Anya ducked behind the counter to put the ledger book away.

Xander's eyebrows shot up in admiration of her negotiating skills. "Well, everything tied up in a neat, tidy package."

"Everything except your toothed fairies," Spike pointed out.

Buffy grimaced. "He's right. Some got away."

"But not that many," Dawn said. "I mean, maybe they won't be able to kill anybody now that there are so few of them. Maybe they'll just hunt pigeons or rats."

"We can only hope," Buffy said.

Willow bit her lip. "Still, we all saw how small problems can turn into oogey big ones."

"Right," Spike said. "Better to nip things in the bud and what all."

"Ooh, bad thought," Willow said. "Anya, you said these things are migratory, right? What if now that they know where Anya lives and where the Hellmouth is, I mean, what if they come back every year like, you know, swallows to Capistrano?"

Buffy raised an eyebrow and looked at Spike. "They're not the first vamps that ever got away. If they ever come back, we'll just have to deal. Meanwhile, it's business as."

"You patrolling tonight?" Dawn asked.

Spike shot the Slayer a challenging look. "Word on the street has it there's a couple of Zugrath demons in town."

Buffy's green eyes regarded him with interest.

"Which ones are those again?"

"Large as elephants and stupider than a sack of anvils," Giles supplied.

Buffy tilted her head to one side and smiled. "Suddenly sounds very wholesome and appealing. Who's coming with?"

About the Author

Rebecca Moesta is the daughter of an English teacher/author/theologian, and a nurse—from whom she learned, respectively, her love of words and her love of books. Moesta, who holds an M.S. in Business Administration from Boston University, has worked in various aspects of editing, publishing, and writing for the past eighteen years and has taught every grade from kindergarten through college.

Moesta is also the author or co-author of more than twenty-five books, including the award-winning *Star Wars: Young Jedi Knights* series, which she co-wrote with husband and *New York Times* bestselling author, Kevin J. Anderson. A self-described "gadgetologist," Rebecca enjoys travel, movie-going, and learning about (not to mention collecting) the latest advances in electronics.

For more information on Rebecca Moesta or her husband, Kevin J. Anderson, see their Web site: *www.wordfire.com*